THE MIND WITH A THOUSAND FACES

An Adventure in Self-Empowerment

Manuel Lanz

Art of Intuition Press

ISBN   978-1-7369442-2-6

Library of Congress Control Number: 2021907073

Published by

Art of Intuition
30751 El Corazón unit 231
Rancho Santa Margarita, California 92688
USA
www.artofintuition.net

Art cover by Manuel Lanz

Pen and Ink Line Art by Marcela Ewertz

To You, The One in all,
for making the completion of this work possible.

The Mind With A Thousand Faces

"On the cosmic scale, only the fantastic has the possibility of being true."

(Pierre Teilhard de Chardin)

THE READING of the COFFEE CUPS.

The story life is telling us is a mystery; some can unconsciously live with the consequences of their choices, while others can create the circumstances for the life they wish to experience.

The Robinsons' Estate had been featured in the Summersville International Realty publication. The Robinsons' empire included: Boat Carriers and Information Technology with the use of Artificial Intelligence. The conglomerate was impressive.

Shivon, the young heiress of the Robinsons' fortune, celebrated her 25th birthday with her guests. The night was summerlike, with a pleasant temperature and light music in the background. As she walked with her friend Ariana near the property's front, they overheard the concierge dismissing a caller at the door in a rather harsh manner.

"What's going on?" Shivon asked him.

"It's a homeless lady begging for something to eat," he replied. "She is offering to read coffee cups to your guests in exchange for food," he added in a mocking tone.

"Give her a warm meal, and thank her for offering her services, which won't be necessary tonight."

"Are you sure? What if it were fun!" Ariana appealed. "Let her in; give her a chance."

Shivon gave in. She instructed the concierge to guide the lady to the powder room and bring her to the library afterward.

"This better be good. Since you interceded for her to stay, now be the first to have a reading; depending on how it goes, you decide if she stays or not."

At the end of her session, the studio door opened, and Ariana walked out. All guests had been waiting and now watched her in silent expectation.

"Next, please," Ariana called out with a smiling face.

The young guests took turns to have their reading by the fortune teller, and one by one, came out with a beaming smile from the session. "She is good! Incredible!"

Shivon, intrigued by her guests' comments and reactions, decided to try a session for herself.

The two women sat face to face in silence. Shivon glanced over the raggedy figure across the coffee table, uncertain as to what to expect from this nonsense.

"I am Shivon."

"I am Elisa; glad you decided to come in."

"Are you a psychic? Can you truly see into people's lives? Please tell me the truth; I would not discredit you with my guests." Shivon's tone of voice inspired trust.

Elisa reflected for a moment and confided: "I don't have a roof, I barely manage to eat one meal a day, I do what I need to do to survive. I tell people what they want to hear; I keep an eye on their body language and listen to their keywords. You see, it's been years of practice. I don't mean to deceive; I just want to be reassuring and offer some hope."

Shivon acknowledged what she had suspected about Elisa's lack of psychic abilities and nodded in a sympathetic gesture.

"There's something I would like to point out," Elisa remarked. "Most of my clients come to me usually driven by curiosity, or just for leisure, therefore my practice works; however, there are instances when the person has a real need for guidance. In those cases, something inside me works differently than my usual self. It is hard for me to explain it with words. I step aside and allow a flow of thoughts and words to be expressed through me, directly from an inner source beyond my control. What comes out in those instances can be trusted."

Shivon attempted to comprehend this revelation; she was also intrigued by the shift in personality from the uneducated, homeless person she had been dealing with to the now articulate, insightful one.

"I didn't come to you for fun or out of curiosity," Shivon clarified. "Is there something I should know?"

Elisa looked aside, unsure, and replied in a subdued voice: "I don't know…. It's not up to me…"

Shivon softened her attitude and stared at Elisa with childish expectation. "I know it's up to you; you just don't know it yet."

After a while, Elisa's gaze became fixed into the void… "You are about to meet a challenge:" Her voice then changed into a deeper pitch. "You will develop a disabling illness, wherein you will not be able to take care of yourself," she stopped and came out of her trance.

"What are you talking about? I am healthy; I feel fine!" Shivon refuted.

" No matter how, it will still happen," Elisa assured her.

"Why? it sounds unfair!"

"We come to this world to comply with a *theme*," Elisa clarified.

"I don't understand!"

"It's not voluntary at the human level; otherwise, how do you explain the assassination of President Lincoln, Gandhi and Martin Luther King? What can you say about Stephen Hawking having to spend most of his life as a person with quadriplegia in a wheelchair? None of us understand the challenges we face during our lives; all I can say is that sometimes we need to endure a trying experience, and in the process of overcoming the hardship, we grow wiser and stronger into better versions of ourselves."

"I hate the idea! I reject the thought of it!"

"Your reaction is understandable," Elisa settled. "For now, I won't talk about it again."

"Why you? "inquired Shivon. "Why did you come into my life to spread these cards on the table?"

"It's the MIND WITH A THOUSAND FACES," Elisa remarked.

"Who is the mind with a thousand faces?"

"I am, you are, we all are. *The ONE became many, and the many are ONE.* I am right now acting like one of those thousand faces; each one of us is an individual expression from the same Source; however, guidance can come in a myriad of modes: from a child, from a barman, a dog, even from a sign on a bench." Elisa spoke with a softer voice. "Source has also been referred to as:

"Ever present, never twice the same, ever-changing, never less than the whole."

The Tent on the Freezing Prairie

There was a discreet knock at the door as Elisa and Shivon were ending their session.

Shivon was surprised to see her brother, a big, strong man in his mid-thirties when she opened the door.

"Sorry, I don't mean to intrude. Do I stand a chance to participate in this event that has your guests raving about before the night ends?

"This is my brother, Arthur," she introduced him to Elisa. "Don't let his appearance intimidate you, he's not as tough as he looks," Shivon joked as she left the room.

"I'm glad to meet you." Elisa greeted him.

"You have a growing fan club in Shivon's guests," Arthur commented with humor. "Your reputation is increasing with each reading."

Elisa returned a gracious smile, then, after a short pause, asked him: "Do you have any questions for me?"

"I'd like to switch gears if it's fine with you. Would you agree if I do the talking while you listen? I promise not to take long."

"Go ahead."

"I'm a soldier in the special forces, and I can't reveal details or locations of my missions, so I will narrate just the point in question:

"About two years ago, I was by myself in the middle of

nowhere trying to stay warm inside a tent. It was late at night, and a freezing wind kept whistling furiously. My best option was to fall asleep and disregard my circumstances. If I snuggle up, I'll save body heat, I thought, and after some time, I experienced that comforting warmth. Still, a funny sensation made me raise my head, only to find a dirty, shaggy, black dog cuddled by my side! Hey, you! Get out! Out! The mutt took a leap, startled, and got away from the tent.

"I did my breathing exercises to induce myself back to sleep, and as I was in this state of low tension, I sent away any thoughts from entering my mind… Not much time had gone by until heavy raspy snoring awoke me to see this warm bag of fleas again by my side. This time I got up in haste, grabbed a shoe, and whacked the heck out of this intruder on the loin. The dog ran away, howling, scared. My heart was pounding, and I was exhausted. The wind had intensified, and it was a punishment to be out there. Then I pondered: What is this old, shaggy dog guilty about? The poor beast was only trying to survive; it just needed shelter from its misery. The mutt was ugly, yet, it was not its fault, and it had as much right to survive as I did. An uncomfortable sense of guilt crept into my heart, so I thought to bring it into safety. I dressed in my bulky winter clothes and walked out of the tent into the sharp wind in a rush. I kept surveying the surroundings, aiming the flashlight through the bushes, only to find that the creature was gone!" Arthur had turned emotional towards the end of his story and remained quiet until he could regain control of himself.

"Thank you for listening; this has been gnawing me inside," Arthur admitted in a feeble voice.

Elisa nodded sweetly in approval and added in a soft voice: "If you look at the path of your life from above, you can see that everything happens for a reason. You said that a sense of guilt crept into your heart. That's because you felt the connection with your spirit in your heart, not in your mind. Guilt prevents you from loving yourself. If you don't love yourself, you don't love others. Guilt opposes love. Spirit comes to the rescue by adopting many forms. This is what I refer to as THE MIND WITH A THOUSAND FACES, in this case, represented by the dog. Spirit respects our freedom of choice; it does not impose. It only suggests and synchronizes the right chain of events for us. In your case, the shaggy black dog was a way for your higher self to show you what compassion feels like, and it's been not until today that you finished this process to become a better Arthur. The dog is fine, and it is affectionately wagging its tail at you from wherever it is.

Two Years Later

Shortly after Shivon's 25th birthday party, she was diagnosed with lymphatic cancer, which had metastasized to several parts of her body. After almost two years of chemotherapy, she had been bedridden for more than three months in one of the most prestigious hospitals near the Hamptons, New York. It had been a gradual, painful process that had deteriorated Shivon physically and mentally. She had become aloof and distant from family members and friends. She hardly ever had any visitors, for they felt unwelcome and opted not to intrude into her trying condition.

"Good morning, miss Robinson," the attending Dr. Hanley greeted Shivon.

She responded with a silent nod.

"How do you feel? You have any news for me?"

"You know how I feel, Doctor; you're holding my latest lab results in your laptop," Shivon replied.

"There's something I'd like to propose to you," Dr. Hanley suggested, trying to sound convincing.

Shivon was silent yet receptive.

"There's a clinical trial for a new drug I think you would qualify for. The initial treatment would last close to three months before we can evaluate any results. It's a new medication that could be helpful in your case; I'm not going to lie to you, the side effects could be severe, but we would do our best to mitigate your discomfort; at this point, I see it as the best option to prolong your life."

"No way! I'm at a turning point in my life; no more treatments! I appreciate your willingness to help me, but the prospect is bleak and not acceptable to me."

Dr. Hanley remained momentarily silent. Then, before leaving the room, he remarked in a kind tone of voice: "I respect the way you feel. Take your time to think about it. I'll be available anytime if you change your mind."

Shivon sighed with relief. She was somehow feeling better this morning. She wandered absent-mindedly around her empty room until she softly focused her gaze on the corridor leading to the doorway in her room; little by little, there was this blurry female silhouette approaching in her direction. Shivon shook her head to come out of her trance-like state to see Elisa standing by the side of her bed.

Shivon's chest was pounding, and sudden tears welled in her eyes, an unexpected reaction beyond her control.

A grinning Elisa, no longer in rags, had arrived looking radiant, healthier, and in excellent shape.

She patted gently on Shivon's shoulder: "I came to thank you for—"

"—Thank me? For feeding you at my birthday party?" Shivon interrupted.

"—for helping me to achieve my purpose in life," Elisa completed the sentence.

"How come?"

"I was on edge, at the end of the line, overwhelmed by adverse circumstances," Elisa confided. "The night of your birthday party, what I started as a fortune teller game for your guests gave me some sense of worth, if only in a playful way at the time."

Elisa now proceeded in a grave tone:

"Nonetheless, the life-changing event was my interaction with you. As I said before, I was overwhelmed with adverse circumstances, forgetful that the ego is not designed to see beyond what your five senses allow you to see. The ego blocks, questions, instigates fear, anger. When you candidly asked me if I had something to reveal to you, your honesty and your pure motive set in me dynamic energies in motion that cleared the channel of communication with my higher self. Ironically, the healer got healed."

Then Elisa added:

"Do you remember the allegory of THE MIND OF A THOUSAND FACES? Well, on that occasion, you acted like one of those faces."

Shivon appeared moved, still recovering from Elisa's unexpected reappearance, and faced her with a curious look: "So tell me, where have you been these past two years?"

"I follow the flow, seeing life as an adventure where I appreciate beauty everywhere I go. Trust and Gratitude are my prevailing mind-set, and I keep an open heart to everyone I meet."

Shivon acknowledged Elisa's veiled answer and conceded not to ask for further details.

"Apart from expressing my gratitude," Elisa continued, "I came here to share essential information with you in this crucial time of your life." She displayed a discrete smile as if she were the bearer of good news.

"Are you trying to cheer me up? I appreciate it, Elisa, but I'm not depressed!" Shivon was emphatic yet not uptight. "I've been informed in detail of the terminal prognosis on my condition. Anyway, before you tell me what you came to share, allow me to express my feelings: For the past three months, I've spent endless days inside these walls, where hope and expectations are so hard to survive. You know that my family has been wealthy for generations, yet wellbeing isn't about money; it's about purpose, about health. My seclusion has made me rearrange my priorities differently; what is real and what is not; what is meaningful, essential, necessary.

Being good is real; trying to be good is not.

Surrender is essential; holding on is not.

This present moment matters; the past does not exist.

What you put out is what you get back.

Shivon paused; Elisa kept listening.

"This morning, my physician offered me an experimental treatment—"

"I know," Elisa interrupted.

"—you may then also know I turned it down."

"Was it because you intend to fight this condition in your own way?" Elisa asked.

"No."

"Are you then giving up? Elisa compelled Shivon to define her conviction.

"I'm not giving up; I'm simply accepting my present condition. The limitations of this illness made me appreciate my life with a new set of values. I'm now convinced that this challenge has been my teacher for the past two years. I accept responsibility for my actions; I'm no longer defensive. I stopped seeking approval from others. More importantly, I have empathy for those in pain or misfortune, and the list goes on!"

Elisa softly patted Shivon's hand, intending to calm her down. "You're making this talk easier for me, as it is what I came to talk with you about. Let me make myself clear: By letting go of fear and recognizing and accepting this painful experience, allowing it to be your teacher, you became immune to this illness; the ailment ceased to have a reason to exist. This morning you assumed a vulnerable position with no resentment or hurt; in doing so, you re-directed your vital energy towards your healing process — energy that you could've otherwise wasted. You don't have to take my word on this, except you have no idea how much healthier you are now!"

Shivon burst into tears. "I do believe you! I do!"

Elisa comforted Shivon lovingly, assuring her that the worst part of her ordeal was over. She praised her spirited disposition and endurance, gradually leading her into a peaceful state of mind.

"There's one crease left that you should iron out," Elisa suggested.

"And what is that?" Shivon asked, beginning to get drowsy.

"You need some rest. I propose a walk in the park tomorrow morning if you feel up to it."

"That would be cool," Shivon mumbled, half asleep.

Elisa kissed Shivon tenderly on her forehead and, in silence, bowed and waved her good-bye.

∼

Transition

Shivon woke up with the feeling that she no longer belonged in this hospital room. Since feeling is the soul's language, she trusted this to be a sign of her improving health.

Elisa arrived early in the morning and requested medical approval for a walk in the park with Shivon on the hospital's grounds.

Rolling in a wheelchair, Shivon appreciated the mild weather and the fresh air as precious gifts. "I'm so happy you're here," she expressed to Elisa. "Are you a master?"

"I'm not the kind of master who has many students, yet I'm certain you're a master yourself, only you have still to realize it," Elisa replied. "You see, students learn from their masters, and masters also learn from their students."

Shivon continued her deep breathing, appreciative of the beauty of the light filtering through the canopy of the trees.

The two women stopped at a secluded area surrounded by trees and bushy vegetation. They found a comfortable spot under the shade of a tree, and for a moment, both enjoyed the calming sounds of nature.

Elisa opened their dialogue: "I acknowledge that you intuitively know to be moving on from an old situation into a new one, and I'm offering to act as a facilitator to assist you in this transition. However, I need your permission —you need to ask for my guidance in this process."

"I do," Shivon agreed. "I trust you."

Elisa continued in a slow, gentle tone: "With your eyes closed, bring your attention to the present moment. For now, leave aside any concerns about your daily life. Set aside this time just for yourself… feeling peaceful on every breath in and releasing any trace of tension on every exhale…in…and…out…Now, allow yourself to remember a time when you experienced significant love, either receiving it from somebody or you giving it to someone. Bring to your mind the place, the time, the circumstances…recall the feeling of this love… feel how it expands and fills every part of your body, realize how grateful you are for this experience…and while being in the soft warmth of this loving state of mind, allow yourself to be paddling on this kayak on a beautiful river in the forest. There are trees on both sides of the riverbank; you realize it's a rainforest far from civilization. You continue to paddle upstream, quietly drifting …and when curving around the next bend in the river, you hear the increasing roaring sound from a great waterfall …All of a sudden, you face it; it's a majestic, powerful torrent…As you get closer, you can feel a gentle spray on your face from the fall's mist…you breathe in this invigorating, cool mist..and before you know, you see this massive wall of water falling with great force…you feel safe, you know it can't hurt you…the high-energy-charged-water is appealing to you… you feel the need to go into this massive shower…you feel this pounding torrent hitting every part of your body…the water is cool and energizing…the force of the water washes out all impurities from your body… FEEL how it clears you to the core, and any traces of cancer are gone… you're fine, you're healthy!

"Now you can turn away from the waterfall, grateful for its healing gift. As you paddle away from the waterfall, you realize that you are in your body, only you are not your body; your heart contains everything you are and everything you own; the love you express and the love you receive is real, your wisdom is real, the link with your spirit is real. As you now open your eyes, you're ready to continue your journey and express and receive love everywhere you go."

"How did you know I needed your help right now?" Shivon asked on the way back to her room.

"I didn't," Elisa answered, "I follow the feeling of the present moment as I identify it is coming from my heart, not from my mind. What I feel now determines my next step and the next. The Inner Self is self-organizing, and as you follow your' hunch,' everything is synchronized for you to be at the right place, with the right people, at the right time to fulfill a purpose."

Shivon felt as if she were returning to her real home, gradually remembering a knowledge she already possessed and had somehow forgotten during her early years of life because of the social conditioning from family members, teachers, and friends.

Once in the hospital room, Shivon implored: "Elisa, please don't leave; I can make arrangements for you to stay as long as you want."

Elisa took Shivon's hands affectionately: "You'll not see me anytime you want, but most likely, our paths will cross anytime you need me."

Shivon turned to her bedside table to open the drawer: "I'm going to give you this special cell phone—" By the time Shivon looked back, the room was empty. Elisa was gone.

The following morning, Dr. Hanley greeted Shivon, wondering what her clinical trial decision had been.

"I've one request before accepting this new drug," Shivon petitioned.

"I'm listening," Dr. Hanley said.

"I'd like to have an updated set of tests to see where my markers are at this point," Shivon asked.

"You know what your recent labs are showing; we just had those results last week," Dr. Hanley disputed.

"I know, I just need to see the most recent numbers before I step into the chamber of torture," Shivon replied, trying to humor Dr. Hanley.

"Alright, we can do it. Just be aware insurance won't cover the tests if we repeat them too soon."

"It's fine," assured Shivon. "I can afford it for my peace of mind."

The Walkabout

Arthur, Shivon's brother, stormed into his sister's room.

"I heard the news! The hospital's director called me to inform me of this turn of events. So, how do you feel? You look fantastic!"

Shivon grinned with satisfaction before her brother's enthusiasm.

"Your physicians can't explain your sudden remission." Arthur embraced Shivon in excitement. "Your doctor wants to keep you under observation for one more day, and then I can take you home." Arthur calmed down and continued: "Our parents are traveling in one of those exotic National Geographic tours, and I don't know exactly in what rainforest on this planet they're right now."

Shivon looked into Arthur's eyes: "You and I haven't talked for quite a while; tell me in all truth how you are." She was aware of her brother's struggle with Post Traumatic Stress Disorder from his past experiences in action.

"I've had better days," Arthur confessed. "Still, the advantage is I'm no longer in the army, and dad is training me to assume his position in the board of directors upon his upcoming retirement." Arthur paused; grabbing Shivon's arm, he pleaded: "Sis, you know I'm not a natural for management. I need you by my side. Your instinct is crucial to deal with the heavyweights. As soon as they release you from the hospital, you can start a new life in our family business. Being together, we can do great!"

Shivon silently admitted that Arthur's proposal made sense. It appeared to be the best immediate course of action to take, yet her inner feeling was like a red-hot resistance wire towards the idea.

Arthur's enthusiasm made her feel sorry for not being on the same page with him. She kept searching for words to explain her position towards the business and what she felt her next step for her life should be.

"Arthur, sit down, and please let me define my current situation: As you're aware, I've been out of commission for the past two years, confined within these walls. My immediate need is 'mobility.' Some people travel for pleasure; some trips allow us to explore, learn, and make us stronger. In my case, I feel my need for 'mobility' as a soul-searching, ritual journey of a spiritual nature. In the Australian aboriginal culture, they refer to it as 'The Walkabout.' While on the move, I need to decide, to create, express, to experience who I AM. What you're proposing to me makes sense; it represents a comfort zone. Nevertheless, my inner call is to escape from the known. My walkabout opens unlimited possibilities; the known would be my trap."

Arthur shook his head, discouraged: "I've no idea what you're trying to say. I know what you mean; only I don't see how this notion applies to you, to us.

Shivon spoke with a serious tone and a gentle expression: "We need to allow each other to walk our paths. Aside from corporate participation, I'll always be here for you if you have a personal need.

Arthur took Shivon in his arms: "I surrender, sis. I still love you. You must be right, anyway. You got the wits, and I got the looks," he joked.

Point of No Return

The private Gulfstream landed in New York in the early afternoon. Edward and Clara Robinson, Shivon's parents, returned from a trip to the Galapagos in Ecuador. Edward Robinson, in his mid-sixties, was a self-made billionaire. He was an unyielding ruler in his family circle. Absorbed by his busy schedule, overseeing his empire, he was hardly available to his family to attend to personal matters.

"Take me to the Hamptons Memorial Hospital," Edward instructed Charles, his driver.

Shivon had been discharged from the hospital and was expecting good old Charles, the driver who had worked for the Robinsons' family ever since she could remember, to pick her up. To her surprise, it was Edward who entered the room, asking Charles to wait outside.

"So, you didn't let cancer get the best of you," he said while greeting Shivon with a bland hug. "I've always said you're tough, the only way to be."

Edward was visibly unsettled, but he tried to act calmly. "Arthur told me your answer concerning my offer to appoint you as a member of the board in our company." Then, he adopted a softer tone: "I hope it was a misunderstanding; you may still have some medication-induced confusion; let's give it some time."

Shivon was mute, frozen with fear. Her father had dominated her during her entire life; Clara, her mother, and Arthur were no exceptions. In the Robinson family, Edward was the boss! A vivid memory in which she was begging Arthur not to enlist for the Middle East fight came to her mind. "I need a breather, sis," he had told her in despair. "I've to get away from this feud."

Now, face to face with her father, Shivon had to stand by her convictions.

"I'm in my right mind, Edward." (She didn't address him as dad). "I knowingly didn't accept the position in the board. To you, I'm expendable; you can hire anybody else in my place. As for me, I need to decide, act, follow my call".

"And what is that?" Edward's jaw tightened.

"You mentioned Arthur had explained my position to you. What else do you need me to add?"

"Are you telling me you intend to go on with your Walkabout?" Edward raised his eyebrows with disapproval. "In Australia, a walkabout is considered to be an excuse to abandon a job nowadays, a way to avoid responsibilities. To make it a valid endeavor, some call it 'Temporary Mobility'— still, carefree time— avoidance of responsibility." His lower lip trembled as he raised his voice in anger.

Shivon's expression sobered; she gazed towards her irritated father and began talking in a gentle tone: "Ever since I was a little girl, I've struggled with constant efforts to gain your approval. Blind obedience shouldn't have been the price for my salvation in your kingdom, but rather a consent offered as a free choice. How do you think I feel knowing you're supposed to love me for who I am, not for what I do?"

Shivon paused, then affirmed: "These past two days, I've been feeling happy for no specific reason; to me, this is an indication that I'm on the right track."

"Wait! Wait," Edward interrupted. "For endless times, you've heard that everything I've taught you has come from my hard-earned lessons. There's no substitute for hard work; we learn through pain and endurance, life is a struggle and a rat race, and the list goes on. Consider all that I've achieved; how can you prove me wrong?"

"I'm not saying you've been wrong," Shivon replied. "We just have different points of view. In your approach to overcome life's problems, you expect your rational mind to find the answers. The point to clarify is that the rational mind gets its information from the five senses. From this limited resource, it attempts to understand how everything is, or how it has been; but the rational mind is not equipped to know how anything will be. This is the function of the Higher Mind, situated at the top of the mountain, so to speak, and can guide us from above to take the best route out of the woods. That's my point; there's a higher level from which we can feel, think, and act in synchronicity to follow the path of least resistance."

Edward remained silent, holding back his outrage.

Shivon gathered strength for her final statement: "You see me as a trained pet, and this little self is now stepping aside to allow my Higher Mind to guide me. I'm not afraid; I'm independent; I'm beneath no one. The essence of our inner self is the source of everything that exists."

Edward burst out in rage: "You give me no alternative! What you need is a wake-up call. I'm going to show you how wrong you are! From now on, you won't receive any financial support from me. I don't expect to see you at home anymore. You'll pack and leave today. I want to see what your beliefs can do for you in the real world. It will be your lesson, or mine. We'll see."

Edward walked out of the room. He was angry and shocked at the same time; Shivon had indeed been his little pet, and he loved her in his way.

"Is there anything I can do for you, Miss Robinson?" a hospital attendant asked Shivon.

"We should never waste energy trying to convince anyone of our point of view," she muttered.

"Excuse me?"

"Sorry, never mind. Would you please call me a taxi?

Symbiosis

As she waited for her cab, Shivon looked around in her room for the last time. She was grateful for the insight she had gained while in pain during her stay in this place.

Her cell phone rang: "The taxi," she assumed.

Instead, her friend Ariana cheerfully greeted her on the line:

"I'm so happy for you; Arthur gave me the good news! I need to see you. Are you available today?"

"For you, anytime."

"Anytime as in now?"

"Sure, I'm at the hospital waiting for a taxi."

"You don't need a taxi! There are so many of us who love you."

"it's complicated. I'll tell you about it."

"I'm on my way; see you in a bit."

In the car, the two friends engaged in conversation. They drove with no specific destination. Ariana listened in disbelief to Shivon's account about the latest turn of events with her father.

"You're right; it is complicated. I don't know what to say."

"I understand; my situation isn't your problem."

"Of course it is! You're my best friend! We've walked so much mileage together, and I'm here for you, unless…"

"Unless what?"

"Unless you want to get rid of me." Ariana laughed.

They both decided to stop for lunch at a pleasant inn by the Hudson River.

"There's news I'd like to share with you." Ariana confided. "My parents changed the terms of my trust, most likely 'based on my good behavior,'" Ariana joked. "I now have full control of my funds, on both the income and the capital. I've been doing some research on investments. It appears the best option would be to buy land, either in Canada or Australia — may be in both. Since we're next door to Canada, I'd like to explore some options as soon as possible.

"Time is of the essence. A contingency clause for the funds' release specifies that I need to allocate a portion of the capital in a conservative investment within 60 days.

"You have a good instinct for investments. Could you come with me on this search? It would mean the world to me. What do you think?"

"It's not about what I think; what's important is how I feel about it, and of course, I feel good about it!" Shivon responded with a playful wink.

IKAN

There was no smog in Lennox. The warm air and sparkling open sky were an invitation to fly, giving the wide-open feeling one can only experience at those heights.

On that glorious day, a small Cessna was flying over the forests of Lennox.

Everything appeared simply perfect on such an afternoon, yet the pilot's face looked tense, and his expression indicated an upset, emotional state. Besides the noticeable annoyance shown on his face, there were traces of violence. Bruises disfigured his well-defined facial features. At 32, Ikan Stolls was athletic and good looking; he possessed a distinctive and magnetic personality, now obscured by his mental state, caught by contradiction.

There are days when everything appears to go wrong, and if one's attitude goes with it, a series of adverse events seem to link together. Ikan already knew this, but he didn't do anything about it, and the consequences soon manifested.

The steady hum of the engine became suddenly interrupted by a prrr...prrr... sound. Ikan quickly pulled on the choke, with no result. He repeatedly stepped on the accelerator, but all the same, the engine kept stalling out. Instinctively, he glanced at the area over which he was flying but couldn't find a suitable place for an emergency landing; the terrain was mountainous and heavily forested. He noticed a clearing in the distance, only the plane had already lost altitude, and the spot now appeared too far to reach.

The foliage was getting closer, and there were no options to take. Frightened, Ikan tried to control the plane, to raise its nose, but the branches were already ripping the aircraft's wings, and the noises grew deafening as the plane tore into pieces.

With the collision, Ikan no longer had any notion of the thoughts that had kept him troubled. Like a sleepwalker, he stood up amidst the rubble and drowsily began to walk off, following the path where the ground seemed to offer the least resistance.

After a while, he couldn't remember how far he had walked, for all that effort had left him exhausted, and he had started to lose his vision. 'Why should I keep walking?' he thought. 'Where to?' He didn't know it, but he felt the impulse of this inner voice that encouraged him to be strong: another step, just one more step. By the time he reached a clearing in the woods, he was exhausted and unable to discern whether what he saw was a mirage or not.

Before him, some fifty yards ahead, there was a rustic cabin. Ikan took slow steps until he reached the door, wearing out his last reserves of energy; without the strength to knock and wait, he opened the door and collapsed.

After a while, Ikan started to move in the state of sleepiness that precedes awakening; he stretched, then "Oh!" Every part of his body was in pain. Slowly, he started to regain consciousness until he could open his eyes. Where was he right now? Although he was practically unable to move any part of his body, he felt peace and had no worries whatsoever. The first images his sight captured were some candles around and above his head, captivating flames that made him feel comfortable.

To his right, he saw a woman of age, watching him kindly. Her affectionate attitude made him feel protected. He was impressed by her slim, straight figure. There were no unpleasant signs of age on her face, her slightly silver hair tied together at the back of her head.

"How do you feel?" she asked.

"I feel fine but confused. Where am I?"

"You're in a safe place in the middle of the forest."

"Who are you?" Ikan asked.

"I'm Elisa; it's a long story. In time I'll tell you about it. Would you like to have some tea?"

"Yes, please."

"Before I tell you my story, would you mind telling me why you feel confused? Aside, of course, from the fact that you're in the middle of the forest with a stranger."

"Well, even though I don't know who you are, I feel like I can trust you. It's as if I've known you all my life. To answer your question, I feel confused because, in recent times, I've been experiencing a series of negative events for no apparent reason."

"I know what you mean. Sometimes it's hard to know the reason for the events we experience in our present time. In those instances, we need to search for its cause in our past."

"I already did that, but I didn't find any explanation," Ikan emphasized.

"Maybe you didn't go back far enough. You need to remember everything. Would you like me to assist you in remembering?" Elisa offered in a sincere tone, "you don't have to share your recollection; it's your private life."

"Yes, I appreciate your help" Ikan sighed in relief.

Elisa started talking in a soothing voice:

"Close your eyes …relax each part of your body… your lips …your eyelids… focus your attention at the point between your eyebrows and relax your mind …" With her forefinger, she gently touched Ikan's forehead.

"Now go back in time… you may remember your college years… however, I want you to go back further …do you remember the time you received a huge puppet at the age of 3? What was its name? I believe it was Tuno, wasn't it?"

He nodded his head yes in a deep state of relaxation.

"Very well …now continue to go back even further …to the time before you were born. You need to remember your assignment, your purpose to accomplish in this lifetime… go back slowly… take your time."

Ikan kept going deeper and deeper in his state until a sudden flashbulb memory came to his mind. His objective to fulfill this life became clear, immediately descending into a gigantic spiral as he fell into deep sleep..

The flames from the candles were again the first images Ikan perceived. It felt like being back home, his comfort zone. He sighed and turned to Elisa, who remained by his side.

"I thought you were just a dream; I felt as if I were somebody else having the experience… somebody other than myself."

"Your impression is understandable," Elisa acknowledged. "We as multidimensional beings function at various levels at the same time. It isn't easy to understand the concept from our rational perspective, which is the overall awareness level in our daily life. From this level, we're unaware of the function of the higher mind, except in those instances when we have a flash of intuition that guides us to the next course of action we need to take."

Ikan pondered over Elisa's explanation:

"I now understand you guided me to a higher level of awareness to be able to recall my purpose to accomplish in my life."

"That's right, and it pleases me you resolved it."

"You assured me I didn't have to share my recollection with you."

"It is private if this is what you wish."

"I need to talk about it with you," Ikan confided.

"It's your choice. I'm listening."

"I'm a scientist. I know the areas of electricity, magnetism, and biology. As a child, my teachers were astonished by my science projects. I studied by myself and did my research. I found the teaching pace in my classroom slow and tedious. I had the feeling that my school was a prison where my parents sent me for just being a child. I will spare you the details.

"Recently, I was working in a power plant, and I'd signed a confidentiality agreement whereby I couldn't divulge the nature of my research. I'll confide in you and tell you that I discovered a way to transmit wireless electricity. This modality would render the current electric power infrastructure obsolete. It would adversely affect the investors in this sector. They threatened me to stop my project. I didn't comply; I continued with my research, and one day two individuals attacked me in my lab. I'd have been beaten to death had I not been rescued by two security guards.

"While flying on my plane, I resolved to forget about science. To retire to a remote place and live off the grid."

Ikan remained reflective as if he struggled with an internal conflict.

Elisa asked: "Those resolutions you had made while you were on your plane… were they validated by what you became aware of during your regression?"

"No. I realized I must follow my passion. I need to channel scientific innovations for the benefit of the world; in a way, it's what I was trying to do, only I encounter resistance from those whose interests are adversely affected by change."

"We live in a dualistic world," Ariana elaborated: Positive, negative; hot, cold; assistance, resistance. There will always be opposing forces. On the other hand, our socioeconomic system in our overpopulated world has become unsustainable. There have to be substantial changes; your innovations will play an essential role in those changes; that is your task."

~

Ariana and Shivon crossed the border with Canada and drove towards Toronto.

"What type of property do you have in mind?" Shivon asked.

"I'd like something surrounded by nature, preferably avoiding densely populated urban areas. I know it doesn't seem like the most profitable investment; yet, equity appreciation isn't my priority for now."

"Where do we start?" Shivon asked, feeling already involved in the project.

"My lawyer suggested Sotheby's or Christie's, but in my college years, I met Max; we became friends, and now he operates his real estate agency. He's doing well, and since I trust him, I'd like to contribute to his success."

Next morning, Max, an enthusiastic salesman, showed an elaborate display of properties to the young women, informing them of prices, statistics, and photographs; in brief, presenting an astounding number of options. Ariana, somewhat overwhelmed, requested a break, and with her hand, motioned Shivon to walk with her out of the office.

"I appreciate Max's effort, but this is making me sick," Ariana held her head with her hands. "Please apologize on my behalf, and tell him something urgent came up, and I'll be in touch."

"Then, what do we do next?" Shivon asked.

"We'll see; something will come up."

~

Ikan had a fast recovery under Elisa's care. While they shared some tea, he leaned back in his chair and clarified:

"I don't mean to sound skeptical, yet, after a few days from my accident, now feeling more robust and alert, I'm having second thoughts about my recent experience with past regression.

"You explained to me we're multidimensional beings, and we function at various levels; don't take me wrong, I can accept that I have a soul, however—"

Elisa interrupts him: "—You're not a human being with a soul; you're a soul having a human experience in a physical body."

"Why would my soul want to have a human experience?"

"The rationale of this is beyond our understanding. Only Source knows why. I'll give you a simple explanation in an attempt to clarify it.

"The Spiritual Realm is a timeless state; hence it cannot experience change. In the process of creation, the universe is continually expanding, evolving. Spirit experiences itself by incarnating in the physical world to overcome limitations: plants adapt to changing climate conditions to survive, and so do animals. As for humans, the challenge is more complicated. As soon as we satisfy our basic needs, we continue our improvement by imposing new limitations on ourselves.

"During childhood, you learned how to ride a bike by using training wheels. At some point you could ride without them, later you became an advanced rider and tried a new challenge, you told your friends: look, no hands! And there were the daring ones who stood on their bike's seat, others, who could do a balancing act by riding on their heads. Do you understand what I'm trying to explain?

"Take, for instance, the man at the circus in his knife-throwing act, using a 'target girl' standing against the board. At some point, the act itself becomes automatic; therefore, a new limitation needs to occur: now he'll do it blindfolded!

"The couple in the flying trapeze decides to perform the double backflip this time without a safety net, and the list could go on.

"To overcome limitations is the objective of the soul in a human experience; if we run out of challenges, we create them!

"As to how to act from the Higher Mind level, I owe you an explanation for a future talk. Now please allow me to have a cup of tea and put my feet up."

~

Ariana and Shivon drove in silence through the streets of Toronto.

"Turn right at the next intersection?" Shivon asked.

"That Avenue will take us out of the city," Ariana pointed out.

"We are almost there; I seem to remember a rustic spa I visited years ago."

After a short drive, they arrived at a charming place with a Zen Labyrinth and a Koi Pond.

"We'll see; something will come up," Shivon reminded Ariana. "Have you thought about any options?"

"Nothing so far. Could you also put your mind to it? Let me know if something turns up."

Shivon strolled in the Zen garden at daybreak, halted under a red maple tree, and sat in meditation. After a couple of hours, Ariana became restless, and walked up and down at the entrance hall.

Shivon appeared unexpectedly, walking peacefully.

"What would I give to be as calm as you are!" Ariana stated. "Lucky you aren't being under pressure for running out of time to comply with the terms of a contract."

"Just as you requested me, I've been trying to find options and may have a lead; let me know when you're ready."

"They serve breakfast in the garden grounds; we may find a quiet spot there," Ariana suggested.

Shivon placed the empty cup on a plate and started talking in a pleasant mode:

" I'm aware that time is of the essence, and you don't have a solution yet. You're tense. Usually, the first reaction would be to dialogue with your mind and analyze your options; the problem is that the mind creates more questions than answers; you become stressed until finally, fear holds you back.

"While I was in meditation, my brain stopped analyzing. I don't mean I was idle; I simply stopped to dialogue with my rational mind. I aimed to reach the silent presence inside of me by becoming an observer and, in a heightened state of awareness, perceive reality beyond the senses. It is about to intuitively know in which direction our internal compass is pointing, rather than expecting to know what our destination is. Once you know this, you move forward with confidence into the unknown."

"My dear friend, you're frightening me! You're not the Shivon I've known all these years."

"I know." Shivon agreed. "I didn't intend to judge you or tell you what to do; the choice is always yours. I appreciate your patience in allowing me to explain my position to you. For what it's worth, I've got a hunch; nonetheless, it's your decision, and I'd take no offense if you didn't want to hear about it."

Daybreak was stimulating in the woods. There was vitality in the air and harmony in nature. Ikan talked to Elisa while rocking on his chair:

"I kept thinking about my conversation with you yesterday. I don't wish to appear close-minded or ungrateful; as I mentioned to you, I'm a scientist; I base my conclusions on numbers and analyze whether anything can be weighed, measured, or detected on the electromagnetic spectrum.

"Nonetheless, your 'simplistic' explanation, as you refer to it, made me consider the possibility of a reality which exists beyond our senses.

"A few months back, I interrupted my research on what is known as 'Dark Matter,' to concentrate on finding the element that links the visible world with the invisible. You may ask: why is this relevant? Well, if the link were found and understood, it could be the way to access another dimension, a parallel universe that oscillates at a different frequency than ours.

"In my latest experiments, I was able to transfer microscopic particles to the so-called 'other side.' I surreptitiously used limited resources from the power plant I worked at, and I was surprised by my success in the last experiment.

"The European Organization in Nuclear Research, CERN, located at the border of France and Swiss, has been working to find portals of access to other dimensions since 1998. More than 100 countries support the research, funded with billions of Euros. It's the largest world project of what could be viewed as science fiction, and yet it's only known by very few people."

Ikan broke off and stared at Elisa.

"I should stop being too technical! I don't want to bore you! Individuals like me don't go to parties; we don't know how to dance. I haven't even had time for a girlfriend!"

Elisa grabbed Ikan's arm with both hands.

"You wouldn't bore me, not for a minute! I love the time we live in, and what you do is fascinating!"

≈

Ariana had conflicting feelings. On the one hand, she saw the Shivon she had known since childhood, the always trusted friend. And on the other, she now faced a new version of Shivon's individuality, which expressed a new belief system utterly unknown to her.

"I apologize if you perceived an abrupt change in my personality." Shivon clarified. "You feel pressed with time, and I've been trying to find options to assist you. Allow me to explain:

"As of yesterday, there was no need to analyze the properties Max presented us since the prospect turned into a stressful situation for you. Fortunately, I'm offering you my gut feeling, which can be trusted. I know that the way I talk to you seems not to stand on solid ground, yet all I can say is that I'm following the same internal guidance that liberated me from my illness while being hospitalized."

Ariana sensed sincerity in Shivon's words. Somehow, she got reacquainted with her old friend.

"I understand, thanks," Ariana admitted, "where do we go next?"

~

Ikan, pensive, gazed into the woods and lamented:

"I lost my job; however, what worries me most, is I'm not allowed to access what used to be my office. I can't retrieve the data on my experiments from any of my notes; they probably destroyed all of it."

"Indeed, they might have destroyed the paper and erased your hard drives," Elisa conceded, "yet, the information is still inside you. Nobody can destroy it."

"But there are too many numbers, formulas, and I don't remember all the details."

"Everything that happens in the universe is permanently recorded. Nothing is lost. In India, they know it as the Akashic Records. They comprise every human event, including thoughts, words, and emotions. Only an authentic clairvoyant can access the Akashic Records. However, in your case, you can recall your information whenever you need it."

"Again, you make me feel out of my element. Nonetheless, I like what I hear about being able to continue with my research with your help," Ikan answered.

~

Ariana and Shivon drove with no specific destination through the woods in the Lennox area.

"Do you have any idea where we're headed?" Ariana asked from the driver seat tactfully so as not to interrupt Shivon's intuitive process.

"No, but we're on the right path," she answered while squinting to keep her concentration.

Ariana was committed to being patient and had chosen to feel the peace and appreciate the beauty in the forested landscape. In an open space by the road, they saw the entrance to a water park. Close by, on one side of the road, a sign read: Metropolitan Oncology Clinic. Shivon asked Ariana to pull out of the road and asserted:

"We need to visit this place."

"The park or the clinic?" Ariana asked. "The park is closed. It's not operating."

As they walked into the clinic, they came across a middle-aged woman in a white gown.

"Can I help you?"

"Good morning; we're not visiting the clinic in connection with its services. We would like to contact the owners of the property. Do you know if both the water park and the clinic belong to the same complex?"

"They do." The woman confirmed. "My name is Nancy Aldrin. I'm the Administrative Director of the clinic. If you come to my office, we can talk more about it."

They followed the woman to her office, and on their way, while walking through the hospital corridors, they noticed some aching patients in their rooms.

"Are you sure we need to see this place?" Ariana asked, unable to hide her apprehension.

"Absolutely, trust me," Shivon whispered.

"May I offer you something to drink?" Nancy asked. "We have an excellent tea shipped to us from Bali."

"Sounds lovely," Ariana answered as both girls nodded in acceptance.

"So, what brings you here?" Nancy asked.

"We're investors looking for a 'green' property. We prefer to have our money invested in the old fashion way, land and bricks, rather than showing an account balance in some digital network."

"History repeats itself," Nancy commented jokingly. "My grandmother used to say that progress is defined by trying to keep everything as good as it used to be in the past." The three agreed and smiled.

Nancy verified some information on her computer screen.

"Magno Nickles is the owner of this property. It is an Australian consortium. They operated the water park for only one year, and even though the place was doing well, they decided to close it for reasons unknown to me.

"The Canadian Metropolitan Hospital decided to transfer its Oncology Clinic to this site and signed a lease agreement with the Australian group. I'm printing the information so you can contact them directly.

"If you allow me a few minutes for an errand I need to make, I'll gladly show you around the clinic. In the meantime, make yourselves comfortable; should you want some more tea, press this button."

Before long, Ariana told Shivon she was going to the restroom and stepped away.

In the meantime, Shivon enjoyed her tea, calmly holding her cup with both hands. She reflected on this new venture under the impression that they were making progress in their quest.

A small face peeked in from the threshold of the door; a pair of big eyes filled with curiosity fixed on her every move.

"Hello!" Shivon greeted the child with a welcoming smile. A little boy about five years old, totally hairless, his fragile body underdeveloped for his age. The tiny figure took the greeting as an invitation to enter the room. Without inhibition, he came close to Shivon and glanced upward to meet her gaze; with a significant effort, he stretched his arm upwards as if trying to touch her hair. The child made a grimace intended to be a smile, then unexpectedly, he closed his eyes and dropped to the floor like a puppet without strings. Shivon, in shock, looked at the tiny figure motionless at her feet.

In despair, she went out to the corridor and cried for help. A doctor showed in no time.

"It's Lucas! He's not breathing!" two medical assistants rushed him to the intensive care unit.

Shivon remained alone in the room, trembling in shock. Unaware, she had sensed the decreasing vital energy in Lucas's last moments. Such an impression had reminded her of the way she had felt in her terminal condition only a few days back. She began to experience chills, hot flashes, her temples drumming to her fast heartbeat. She wondered: Am I really in remission? Have I been restored to health? Her breathing was getting shorter, a buzzing set in her ears, then an intense burst of dizziness and finally blackout.

$$\sim$$

Elisa approached Ikan, who was getting ready for his imminent departure.

"I need your help." She seemed to be uneasy. "Could you drive my old jeep to take me to a medical clinic not far from here?"

"Are you Ok?" Ikan reacted apprehensively.

"I'm fine. I promised my help to someone who needs it right now."

The Jeep arrived, screeching to a halt at the entrance of the clinic. The reception desk informed Elisa and Ikan; they could not visit Shivon since they were not related to the patient. Elisa debated that Shivon wasn't a registered patient in the clinic; therefore, the blood-related rule didn't apply; she claimed to be Shivon's close friend and insisted she urgently needed her support. The receptionist called the physician in charge, and the visitors were authorized to have access to the premises.

Elisa held Shivon's hand; she was sleepy as if wishing to evade a sad reality.

"Shivon, it's me, Elisa… I'm here for you… I care about you… you are safe… I'll be here… rest."

After sleeping for a while, Shivon opened her eyes:

"I thought I saw you in a dream."

"I heard a similar comment from somebody else a few days ago."

"What happened? Why are we here? Shivon asked as soon as she regained consciousness.

"What's the last thing you remember?" Elisa asked.

Shivon's expression turned tense as she remembered the traumatic event.

"How is the child?" she asked, agitated.

Elisa held her close with affection and explained:

"Listen to me, sweetheart; little Lucas accomplished his life purpose in the physical world; it was his time to move on. The witnessing of his transition impaired you beyond your emotional control. It was an unexpected event. The fact that it took you by surprise made you recollect the worst stage of your illness, just days ago. Lucas is right now out of harm's way, and you have a long road ahead.

Elisa lowered her voice in a solemn tone:

"Please listen to what I need to tell you:

"Your mindful state of awareness shouldn't be limited to your meditation sessions. You should maintain your spiritual awareness 24 hours, seven days a week. It is the only way you can be in a receptive state to attract the positive events you wish to experience in your life.

"Remember that fear is an emotion; energy charges emotion, and energy manifests your reality. You know these concepts, don't be caught off guard!"

"You're right, Elisa, the little one's helpless state crushed me; It took me by surprise. Now I realize you can be compassionate, as well as empathize with somebody's condition without undermining yourself."

A nurse walked in, requesting the visitors to walk out to check on the patient.

While in the visitor's area, Ariana had been keeping an eye on Elisa. Her face looked familiar to her, except she didn't remember who she was. Elisa felt stared at by Ariana and approached her:

"I'm glad you attained your objective."

"Do you know me?" Ariana felt exposed.

"I couldn't say I know you, yet I remember our conversation."

"I'm sorry, where did we meet?"

"Does the reading of the coffee cups night ring a bell?"

"Are you …? Really?" Ariana responded with surprise and embarrassment for not recognizing her earlier.

"I apologize; I'm not good with faces, even though I clearly remember our conversation. How do you know I attained my objective?"

"Somebody said: If you want to learn something, teach it. Can you explain to me how you managed to achieve your goal?"

Ariana started her narrative:

"I've always had my material needs covered; nonetheless, when I met you, my life was uneventful. Internally I had an enormous amount of energy, building up pressure like a volcano. I needed resources to increase my options, explore new opportunities, meet people, share stimulating experiences in the world. In an attempt to obtain resources, I practiced a mind control method based on affirmations. At that time, you explained that I needed to infuse these with energy for my intention to manifest in my reality; otherwise, assertions are just words.

"You also made me aware that by persisting in my expectation for results, I prevented my intention from happening because the expectation made me remain in the 'I Do Not Have' vibrational state; lack kept manifesting in my reality. Like attracts Like.

"You suggested that rather than being concerned about what I didn't have, I had to be grateful for my many blessings, and you were right! Here I am, with resources at hand and my best friend by my side on our way to see what life has in store for us.

Elisa nodded, pleased by Ariana's comment.

Ariana went on:

"I didn't recognize you so changed: No rags, rested, vibrant expression. May I ask if you were affected by misfortune at the time we met?"

"The night I met you, my life changed. I was a raggedy woman knocking at Shivone's residence in need of help. I'd been devastated by adverse circumstances, unable to realize that I was identifying myself with my problems, my events. The ego is an entity that believes to be separate from spiritual unity. It thinks I am here, and the universe is out there, indifferent to my cries for help; hence: As you believe, so you will experience.

"The reading of the coffee cups night was my wake-up call; it made me conscious of being deceived by a mirage. That night during my interaction with each one of the guests, for each of the questions they presented, I took steps to evaluate my answer silently:

Is it empowering? or it controls.

Integrates? or separates.

Positive? or negative.

Based on love? or in fear.

"You may remember that the consensus at the end of the sessions was positive. The accuracy in my readings convinced the guests, and in the process, I regained my center; I reclaimed my real identity."

A nurse let Elisa and Arianna know they might return to Shivon's room. They noticed she was in much better spirits, convinced she was ready to be discharged from hospital care.

Elisa addressed Ariana and Shivon:

"There's a special person I recently met; he's been my guest and drove me here today. Poor guy! He's been patiently waiting for hours out there in the clinic. I'd like you to meet him. May I introduce him to you?"

They both accepted.

Ikan greeted them and turned to Shivon:

"I'm glad you're back on your feet; you had Elisa worried. I see you're precious to her."

"The feeling is mutual," she answered while glancing at him with curiosity.

After discussing for a few minutes the excellent service the hospital's staff had provided for Shivon, Ariana insinuated:

"It's been a long day, and we need to give ourselves some care and pamper our empty tummies. Would you accept my invitation to dine in a quiet place to get to know each other?"

"Please take me with you!" Shivon laughed. "I refuse to dine hospital food!"

～

The newly acquainted group enjoyed their peaceful interaction at a local Country Inn.

Elisa called for attention:

"Somehow, I've got the feeling that the four of us being together here and now is giving us an opportunity we should seize. I propose that each of you describe the most relevant aspect that comes to your mind in connection with how you experienced Shivon's incident.

"Great idea!" Shivon intervened. "May I suggest Ikan be the first one to talk?"

Ikan, introverted by nature, had a difficult time suddenly becoming the center of attention.

"Mine is a long story. It contains many details concerning my education, places where I resided, and the many changes I went through in my family life. For now, I will focus on Elisa's proposal: to describe the most relevant aspect to come to my mind, in connection with how I experienced Shivon's incident:

"I'm a scientist. I studied at Cambridge University and the Federal Institute of Technology in Zurich, Switzerland, known as Poly. I'm committed to research in several science branches; however, I will refer only to biology in this case.

"During Shivon's crisis today, I spent several hours in the clinic waiting for Elisa. During that time, I observed how the place operated. I saw patients of different ages walking by. I couldn't help but experience empathy for the suffering some of them were showing. Years ago, I did some experiments to study the relationship between emotions and some diseases, which now come to my mind."

Ikan stoped, reflected for a moment, and continued:

"I need to make clear that it is not my intention to create controversy or make negative criticism about something or someone. I started my experiments because I had the impression that medicine in the Western world had focused on treating symptoms with expensive medications and high-tech devices. All the same, in general, it didn't solve the cause of disease. I don't blame anyone, since in some cases, there are no diseases, plainly sick individuals; I'm referring specifically to degenerative diseases or those of the immune system in which viruses or bacteria don't play a role.

"My goal has been to find a solution to eliminate the condition that ails the sick, not just give them palliative care. As you know, we function and move with vital energy, which in China they know as Chi, in India they call it Prana, and in Greece, they name it Ether; the concept is the same and applies to humans, animals, and plants.

"During my research, I worked with a similar device to one that had existed before. I'm referring to the vital energy concentration system built by Wilhelm Reich, an Austrian psychiatrist. It was a chamber big enough to accommodate a human being within it. The procedure consisted of concentrating vital energy in and around the person for approximately half an hour. Depending on the case, they repeated the session for one or two more days. In his book, 'The Cancer Biopathy, ' Wilhelm recounts the remission cases in cancer patients he achieved with his chamber, which he called 'Orgon Accumulator.' The Conspiracy Theory claims that its system's result was such a success it became a threat to the business side of the medical industry. The FDA declared him a quack and locked him in federal jail. They destroyed his notes and equipment, and two years later, when Wilhelm Reich was about to be released from prison, he died in 1957.

"Wilhelm's chamber specifications were lost when his opponents destroyed his studies; however, I decided to work on the same concept. To that end, I set up a small laboratory in Indonesia.

I built my version of the chamber because Wilhelm had used a combination of organic and inorganic elements. After experimenting for some time with plants and animals, I began using the device with humans.

"The result was initially successful. Once the patient had undergone several sessions in the chamber, the process restored the vital energy, and the condition disappeared, leaving the patient cured.

"The problem is that the riddles life challenges us with are not always so easy to solve. Although the chamber I developed was an apparent success, the patient's condition recurred after a while.

"I needed an assistant, so I employed an intelligent elderly man I'd interviewed to give him an opportunity. His name was Ari. One day I became frustrated by not achieving permanent healings with my work; I'd reached a dead end.

Ari came to me and explained in his usual formal approach:

'With deep respect, I would like to mention something about the work you do, and I humbly collaborate in.'

"Of course, Ari! I answered."

'You see me as an opaque solid body. As for me, I can soft focus my vision in such a way that I see you as an electrical circuit with many 'power lines' circulating in harmony throughout your entire system. When somebody generates negative emotions such as frustration or guilt, they block or divert these energy channels. If the negative emotion becomes chronic, the 'disrupted energy' manifests physically, leading to a condition or disease, ranging from a headache to an ulcer or even cancer. The chamber you have built effectively restores the correct course of the energy channels; however, if the patient does not modify their negative emotions or belief system, the pathological condition recurs. Healing must come from within the person's vibratory system.

'Excuse me for giving you this comment you didn't ask for.'

"I was perplexed by his comment. Ari bowed in respect and left the laboratory. I never saw him again. All this happened about six years ago. As a man of science, I didn't know how to move forward. I suspended the energy concentration chamber research. However, I feel that the key points are present, and the work should continue.

"At that time, life led me on a different path. I moved to Chicago, where I've been working in the field of electricity and magnetism. Thank you for listening."

The group was silent. In the mental atmosphere they shared, one could almost feel the brainstorming taking place in each of them, which suggested options, images, projects, desires, and questions in need of answers.

Ariana took the initiative breaking the silence:

"I don't know about you, only that I have an internal revolution of information I need to process. I trust Elisa's instinct that our paths crossed here and now for some reason, and we must continue sharing our comments. At the moment, I propose a break. I will be pleased if you accept my invitation to stay at this inn. I don't think we would find another option nearby where we could all be together in one place."

Elisa raised her eyebrows and mimicked silent applause with her hands. "Excellent decision; tomorrow will be your turn for your comment."

With both hands joined in pranam, she bowed goodbye to everyone.

Ariana

The following morning, the newly acquainted friends joined each other for breakfast in the Inn's garden. An atmosphere of good

mood prevailed. Personal interaction had ruled out formality in exchange for a sense of humor. Ikan was the only one who remained circumspect. His reasoning process, always accurate and literal, tended to interpret comments in a textual way. During the time Elisa had shared with him, she hadn't heard him laugh out loud. Despite this, he was a warm person with empathy for the well-being of others.

The time came for Ariana to offer her comment. The group paid attention.

"My life has had a few nuances. I grew up in an environment of privilege, protected from worldly risks and dangers. Due to their considerable wealth, my parents guided me to study Business Administration; I graduated from New York University Stern School of Business.

"Mom and Dad were lucky. I didn't give them the headaches students usually give at that age. I was calm, avoided alcohol, and didn't experiment with drugs.

"They conditioned me to plan and predictably live my life until… there came a time when I felt I wasn't using my potential. I yearned for new experiences. I needed to overcome obstacles that would allow me to acquire wisdom, become more assertive. At this crucial moment, my friend Shivon entered my scene. She helped me make decisions on what I now see as the right path. I'm an entrepreneur by nature, and I wish to develop a Research and Service Center for human well-being. I feel tempted to suggest it could start in the water park's locality, including the clinic we were in yesterday.

"Before coming to Canada, I did some research work on potential investments and paid some professional consultants for their opinions. Despite this, my planning limited me to just moving from New York to Toronto. In contrast, in the last forty-eight hours, a higher-order has linked a series of events and people, which would have been impossible to plan and to connect in any other way; I mean, look at the four of us here, gathered for some reason; there must be a purpose."

"Thank you for your words, Ariana," Elisa mediated. "You've given us valuable information to consider our options.

Shivon, you're the only one left to give us your point of view. Would you like to comment now?"

She nodded in agreement and began to speak slowly:

"First of all, I want to thank you for the support you've given me during my incident while visiting the hospital. At the same time, I understand that my problem served for the four of us to meet, and for some reason, we're together here sharing our ideas. The comment I can make about my incident is that I am a work in progress; it has served me as a wake-up call not to lose sight of our true nature and our vast potential to overcome the obstacles our daily life presents to us.

"In the last two years, I've experienced a series of health challenges that have led me to introspect and, in turn, have guided me to develop my intuitive capacity. During the time we've been sharing together, I've felt that a purpose with multiple possibilities is taking shape; I only ask you to allow me to be in it. I'm willing to do my best. Thank you."

Elisa glanced at each of them to make sure no one needed to add anything and proceeded to summarize: "I share Shivon's feeling that right here and now, something is taking shape. I suggest we take some time to process the information we've received, and the day after tomorrow, we meet again to see if we have something concrete to propose. It would require the four of us staying here to keep in touch. Who in favor?" Everyone accepted.

They didn't address the subject again. All members attended to their interests for the rest of the day.

The night at the lodge was pleasant with the sounds of crickets and some nocturnal birds. Shivon was contemplative, sitting by a stream. Ikan approached her, somewhat shy, not wanting to disturb the magic of the moment.

"Do I interrupt you if I sit here?"

"Not at all. This place is inviting." She patted on the spot next to her.

"Now that I see the water running, I remember seeing some information at the Inn about a river that runs about a mile away from here. The water is transparent at this time of the year, and there are many varieties of fish. At the Inn, they have diving masks available, and they sell some horrible bathing suits. Tomorrow we have a day off; we could explore the site if you're up to it."

On the riverbanks, the vegetation was lush. The crystal clear water circulated gently. Ikan and Shivon's figures, equipped with diving masks and fins, seemed to float as if suspended in a luminous space. The rays of light filtered in the scene, giving it a surreal look. While gliding in silence, Shivon had the 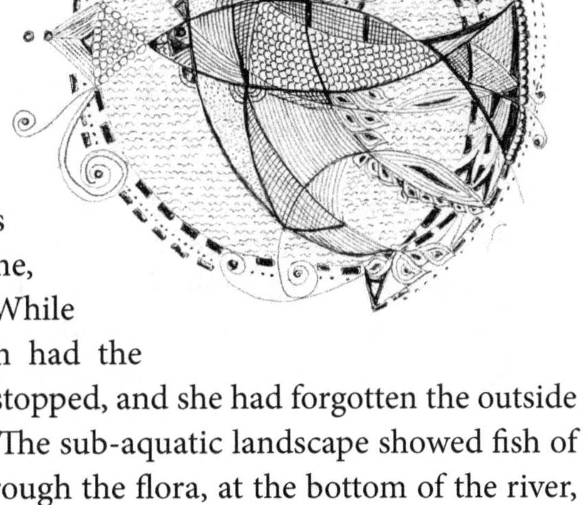 impression that time had stopped, and she had forgotten the outside world's existence entirely. The sub-aquatic landscape showed fish of different varieties, and through the flora, at the bottom of the river, she was amused by seeing crabs popping in and out.

A fallen tree trunk on the water served as a support to take a rest.

"How far does this river go?" Shivon asked, removing the mask from her face.

"I don't know. We've advanced beyond the range shown on the map at the hotel," explained Ikan, "Would you like to turn back now?"

"Not at all! I'm enjoying the variety of underwater landscapes. Would you mind going down the stream for only a few more minutes?" Shivon suggested.

Upon reaching a rocky area, the river took a curve, and something terrifying that the couple of swimmers would have never imagined, unexpectedly happened. Along with a huge rock about eighty feet away, the land abruptly swallowed the current to become an underground stream.

Shivon heard a distant noise, like that of a gigantic strainer. She noticed that the fish swam in the opposite direction of the current. As she drew her head out of the water, she discovered in horror that in a short distance, the force of the river current was about to suck them in.

"IKAN!" she screamed as loudly as she could, but he was underwater and couldn't hear her. As a last resort, Shivon pulled him by the hair, to which he reacted with surprise until he realized the situation; they managed to hold on to some branches on the riverbank and crawled out of the water, over the grass, where they fell exhausted.

They remained silent for a while before recovering from their distressing experience.

Ikan started the dialogue in a positive tone, without referring to what could've happened.

"You saved my life. As you see, today, you had one more challenge to continue with the development of your intuitive level."

"Yes, I did. I'm sorry for having involved you in my ordeal." Shivon was still catching her breath.

~

An Unusual Story

On their way back to the Inn, Shivon and Ikan had hardly crossed a word. After walking for about half an hour, they decided to rest in a peaceful spot by the river.

"Ikan is an unusual name; what is its origin?"

"It's Mayan. My father was Mayan; Ikan Cumatz."

"But your name is Ikan Stoll, not Cumatz." Shivon seemed puzzled.

"My mother was Swiss, Martina Stoll. I use my mother's last name."

"Sounds very original! Mayan father and a Swiss mother. How did they find each other? There must be an interesting story here! I'm fascinated by the reminiscences of how couples met. Would you tell me about your parents?"

"Well, it's an unusual story... I don't know..."

"We have plenty of time, and it's our day off; unless... you consider it private..." She tilted her head.

"I'm not a good storyteller," Ikan apologized. "It's hard for me to color a human saga, yet, you mentioned yesterday that you're a 'work in progress' on your psychic aspect, so my lousy storytelling could improve with your clairvoyance and visualization skills."

"Like the best movie." She raised her chin with pride.

"Ikan began his narration without hesitation:

"My mother, Martina, was a scientist. She specialized in chemistry and biology. A Swiss government agency sent her to the Mayan Biosphere community in Guatemala. The objective was to advise and support the government's effort to protect its forests and wildlife. The locals, burdened by poverty, were burning the forests to plant corn, and the tropical biosphere was disappearing at an alarming rate. My mother could instruct local people giving them alternatives to live off the land sustainably while protecting the trees.

"Her job was complicated and difficult; she had to travel on foot to remote places in the jungle. She depended on Canek, a faithful interpreter who translated the Mayan native language to a bad Spanish. During her explorations, she collected plants with alleged healing properties for further research in scientific form.

"After a year of working in the area, Martina's efforts made it possible to recover many forest areas. The inhabitants had learned to work with the wood in a renewable way and were no longer burning the forests to plant corn.

"Due to the harsh conditions in which Martina worked, she was exhausted, and one day she got sick with a fever. She was in a remote place in the jungle and couldn't move. The Tropical Disease Center prescribed her antibiotics, which failed to resolve her case. The fever didn't give way. Her loyal interpreter, Canek, requested assistance from the local herbalist Ikan Cumatz, and that's how she met my father, a strong man with a penetrating gaze. The local people respected him and held him in great esteem, for he had saved many lives.

"Cumatz examined Martina's trouble to breathe, her chest rising and falling with rapid motions. He confirmed the antibiotics were not effective in controlling the condition affecting her. He asked his assistants to have Martina laid down by a bend of a nearby stream. Then, he instructed her to perform a *pranayama* modality, which consisted of what we currently know as diaphragmatic breathing.

"Cumatz carefully supervised Martina to make sure she could maintain the breathing rate he had indicated. At some point in the exercise, Martina began to experience the fingers of her hands becoming paralyzed. Cumatz immediately instructed his assistants to submerge her in the river's water, with only her face above the surface. After a while, Martina began to feel better. Cumatz helpers carried her out of the water, wrapped her in a warm linen cloth, and placed her in a comfortable position to rest until she recovered.

"By the time my mother felt better, she asked for Cumatz to thank him for his intervention. He was already gone.

"On that same day, Martina received a message from the Swiss center requesting her to return to Switzerland as soon as possible. She told me she was devastated when the agency informed her that her task ended and she needed to go back. She experienced an internal struggle; she knew her job hadn't finished; however, there were profit interests opposed to the protection of the forests.

"One afternoon, before her return to Switzerland, Martina showed up at Cumatz hut:

'I received life-changing unexpected news from my country; otherwise, I'd have come to see you sooner. ' Martina confided, somewhat disheartened.

'Come to see me? Do you feel unwell?' Cumatz asked with discretion.

'Physically, I feel fine thanks to you. It's related to the organization where I work. They ordered me to return to Switzerland; I've integrated myself with this community; I deeply feel that my life covers a purpose here.'

'Think about it: you say you want to act where your service is useful, why don't you let the Creator take care of the details?' Cumatz proposed equanimous.

"Martina felt attracted by the Shaman's animated features. In contrast with his heavy, formal frown, she could perceive tenderness in his gaze.

'I've collected countless plant specimens to use in laboratory studies in my country; If you help in the description of their healing properties, we could save time with better results. If you agreed to come to Switzerland, you would be well paid, and I'd take care of all the arrangements.'

"Cumatz reacted with a measured tone.

'Here, I was born, and here I've lived. Nature has revealed to me many of its secrets. I am useful to my people; they have no doctors or hospitals. Each human group has its task to accomplish, and mine is here.'

Ikan stopped at the representation he was acting in the form of dialogue.

"You're doing it very well! You're an excellent storyteller!" Shivon uttered.

"The part that follows is difficult to understand. Truthfully, I won't be able to reproduce the dialogue because my mother kept it private. In essence, mom explained that she experienced several conflicting emotions the same afternoon she went to see Cumatz. There was no doubt that my mother admired him for his integrity and was grateful to him for saving her life. The spark of intelligence in his expression fascinated her. Simultaneously, she was discouraged because Cumatz didn't want to go to Switzerland, and to leave everything meaningful to her behind filled her with consternation.

"At this level, I don't know the details. The only thing my mother trusted me was her need to take something from this world that had made her so happy. She had never married or interest in looking for a partner; however, she needed to be a mother and wanted a part of that world to go back with her. My mother got pregnant by Cumatz and went back to Switzerland; she kept him as a memory for the rest of her life, for she never heard from him again."

At the end of his story, Ikan noticed Shivon was sobbing silently. He tried to tell her something, except he couldn't find the right words.

"Don't mind me," Shivon apologized, "your story is very moving indeed. Because of it, you're here, and I get to know you."

~

That same night, the phone rang in Ikan's room:

"Hi, Ikan," Ariana's voice, "if you're available, can we talk for a moment?"

"Of course! What can I do?"

"Can I see you in the garden?" Ariana suggested.

"Sure, see you in a bit."

As they strolled by a tranquil pond in the garden, Ariana spoke with a formal tone:

In these past two days, we've known each other better. We have the knowledge and expertise to integrate an efficient work team. We only need to define where we're heading. Tomorrow we'll discuss our ideas and options. I find the research field you're in remarkably interesting. Therefore, I'd appreciate your professional opinion on the investment project I have in mind. Today I started communicating with an Australian consortium. They were open to selling the property. It seems to be an excellent investment; however, my interest is not only profit-oriented. I'd also like to use the facilities to develop a Research Center for public benefit. It could function as a non-profit organization. My question is if you could evaluate the property and prepare a report of its potential for me?"

Ikan remained thoughtful while feeling a flare of enthusiasm.

"Yes, I'd like to do it. How much time do we have?"

"Would a week be enough for you?"

"I think so. Can we comment about it tomorrow at the meeting?"

"Of course, I think it will be good news."

The next day Ariana informed the group about her project's initial plan. The four of them, Elisa, Ikan, Shivon, and Ariana, would be founding members of Konnect, a new non-profit organization.

～

KONNECT

Three months later, Konnect had acquired the property and built dwellings and offices for their members in what used to be the water park.

Ikan called for a meeting and exposed a recent idea:

"We have the Oncology Clinic on our site, and it occurs to me we could propose an alternative therapy for cancer along with the traditional treatment they practice. Do you remember my version of the concentrating energy chamber initially developed by Wilhelm Reich? Well, I've thought of some improvements, and I think we could have good results. I also hope you remember that although the chamber restores the correct course of the energy channels in the human body, it is necessary at the same time to assist the patient in modifying their negative emotions so that the pathological picture doesn't recur. It would be up to Elisa and Shivon to give support to the psychological aspect of the person.

If we agree, we could immediately propose it to the Canadian Metropolitan Hospital."

Time Heals All Wounds

The treatments with the concentrating energy chamber had proven positive. Elisa and Shivon gave supportive therapy to patients with guided meditation, visualizations, and hypnotherapy. Nancy Aldrin, director of the clinic, had not been very enthusiastic about supporting the alternative form of therapy despite its apparent benefits; she stood out of it.

An assistant informed Shivon of a visitor at the reception who claimed to be his brother Arthur.

"Hi, Sis!" He hugged her effusively." You look even better than I saw you last time; as usual, you were right when you rejected my proposal to work in the Robinson consortium. Following your path has been the best decision. I'm not so involved in our company's daily operation, it isn't me, it isn't my personality, but tell me about yourself! Are you happy?"

"I work with admirable people; I'll introduce you to them; one is my friend Ariana, the one you know. I can tell you about the organization we just founded; it's dedicated to research for public benefit. I hope you came with enough available time."

"Sis, for you all the time in the world. I also came to tell you a story; Is this an appropriate time?"

"Sure, I hear you."

"Dad met a young woman during their university time; her name is Teresa. They lived together for a while until there came a time when they realized their relationship would not be the marital type, and they decided to part ways and staying as close friends. Our mother knows dad has maintained an occasional communication with Teresa all these years. They've supported each other in their capacity as confidants, nothing more. Why am I telling you all this?"

Arthur continued:

"Teresa got cancer; her prognosis wasn't very encouraging because it was detected when she was already in the 4th stage. Teresa never married and lives alone. Here comes your part:

"Dad had her admitted to the Metropolitan Hospital two months ago, and Teresa experienced an amazing recovery; they discharged her two weeks ago."

Shivon looked at Arthur in amazement.

"Do you mean Teresa Sullivan?"

"The one and the same Sis, you saved her life in this place! Teresa told Dad in detail about her experience in the chamber. Above all, she expressed herself positively about the guided meditation sessions you gave her. Teresa is aware that she managed to free herself from several adverse events that overwhelmed her with your help. Now she feels free.

"Teresa's healing has radically changed Dad. He's deeply sorry to have cut you off from his life; he doesn't know how to face you. He made arrangements with the lawyers and reinstated you as an heiress in the part that belongs to you; He also reactivated your bank accounts. You know, Sis, I see him older and tired, I don't know if you…?"

"I understand, Arthur, and I appreciate you're telling me this; I'm also grateful Dad is reconsidering. Despite everything, it wasn't me who turned my back on him; if one day he wants to see me, he knows where to find me, and I'll be here with open arms."

"I respect your position Sis," Arthur admitted.

Five months after its inception, Konnect was a thriving organization with office staff and assistant therapists. Ikan had hired some Canadian scientists, and the atmosphere of the place bustled with positive activity.

Ikan called in Ariana's office.

"Do you have a minute?"

"Go ahead, tell me." Ariana closed her laptop.

"I want to bring a topic I consider important:" Ikan began with a measured tone, but seeing Ariana's uptight reaction, he clarified to her: "I warn you we'll enter science fiction grounds."

"What a relief! I thought you had bad news for me." Ariana smiled.

"Fortunately, the alternative therapy program is working at a good pace in the clinic, so I've had the opportunity to prepare what our next project could be."

"What's it about?" Ariana turned toward him.

"It's about the conduction of electrical energy without wires."

"Do you mean conducting electric current as if it were WI-fi?"

"That's right," Ikan nodded. "The concept is lost in the night of time. Modern studies discovered that the Egyptians already used wireless energy conduction. I don't want to take your time with too many technical details. I'll mention only the basics.

"The pyramids of Egypt were not graving as they once believed. They built them with granite and dolomite, which are conductive materials of electricity, and covered their surface with a layer of limestone, an insulating material; consequently, the pyramid acted as a gigantic generating and transmitting source of electric power for its inhabitants.

"Now we move in time and space to 1898; a scientist named Nikola Tesla from Croatia managed to transmit energy also wirelessly. His method was different from that of the pyramids. Still, there were some similarities in. We can delve into the technical details as far as you want, but in summary, I want to inform you is that I've managed to build a prototype using both methods; that of the Egyptians and the Tesla. This morning, from my laboratory, I could wirelessly turn on a spotlight located at the end of our property one thousand feet away."

"What you tell me seems science-fiction indeed! Now tell me the implications your prototype could have for Konnect; for us." Ariana asked.

"I fear the project I propose to you is too big to be handled by us. Can you imagine a world in which you eliminate all power lines? No more cables in the streets or houses. I wouldn't say I like to talk about conspiracy theories; however, when Tesla publicly showed his wireless accomplishments, it meant the end of his career since they blocked him in the scientific and commercial fields. In time he died poor and isolated.

"If you asked me what the implications for Konnect and us are. It would not be easy to go against the current infrastructure installed worldwide."

Ariana felt butterflies in her stomach. She was facing something of a considerable risk in front of her.

"We have to notify our friends about this situation. We need to devise a plan. The scientists you recently hired, do you trust each one of them?"

"Not at this level," Ikan admitted. "This morning I made the experiment in secrecy, without witnesses. My collaborators know part of the theory; nonetheless, I've divided the functions, and none of them knows the whole and final process."

"Sounds good, Ikan! keep it confidential, now more than ever."

During an extraordinary meeting, the group listened to Ariana as she explained Ikan's latest project and its possible implications for Konnect.

At the end, Shivon proposed:

"I'd like to introduce my brother Arthur who I fully trust; his knowledge and contacts would be valuable, and he could advise us in this situation." Next, Shivon explained to the group that his brother belonged to the army's special forces for several years. She didn't know the details of his missions since they were secret; she only knew he was absent for several years and awarded him medals for his services. Arthur had retired from the army and currently worked in the Robinson consortium.

Ariana proceeded to summarize:

"If you agree, I suggest Shivon let Arthur know about the topic we've discussed today, and if he wants to get involved, I hope he can give us his opinion on the course to follow as soon as possible.

"I emphasize Konnect is currently developing two projects: one, the energy storage chamber originated by William Reich and number two, the wireless electric transmission originated by Nicola Tesla. In the past, at the time they exposed both concepts to public light, they caused a tragic end for both researchers; therefore, if we're aware of the risk and wish to move forward, as of today, we must act with caution."

Arthur was uneasy and could not sleep because of the information Shivon had revealed to him. There were multiple risks. It would affect the economic interests of the most influential groups on the planet; security would be an issue; there would be no one to trust.

He decided to go for a walk in the middle of the night. At the end of a tree-lined path, he saw a dim light; his instinct of several years making night guards drove him to look. As he came closer to the building, he saw Ikan through a window totally absorbed as he worked in the still of the night.

He was about to retire with discretion, only he saw two human figures with ropes in their hands that sneaked up behind Ikan. Arthur reacted and ran around the building towards the laboratory. Before entering, he noticed an armored truck parked at the door. In a matter of seconds, he suspected these were two criminals, and the target was Ikan. Upon entering the laboratory, the two armed intruders saw him. From about one hundred feet away, the assailant shot at Arthur, who dodged the bullet and ran for cover behind some shelves. Next to the wall, he discovered a fire extinguisher and launched a jet of chemical dust to the face of the attacker, chasing him before he could shoot at him again. Gunshot noise had alerted two armed security guards, who entered the laboratory, and subdued the attackers.

The next day Ariana addressed the group, this time including Arthur.

"The police inspector in charge of our area informed me the two attackers were common criminals hired by an anonymous source; the goal was to kidnap Ikan."

"Who could want to kidnap Ikan?" Shivon asked.

"We don't know," Ariana admitted. "Someone in our organization is aware of the progress in Ikan's research. We have a spy."

Arthur intervened with emphasis.

"I've decided to accept your offer to act as a consultant for you. I suggest that for a few days no key or substantial progress be made in the experiments currently being performed. I need time to investigate."

The Fraud

Arthur addressed Shivon:

"Sis, would you accept me as a partner in Konnect, even if I worked at the Robinson Consortium? And if so, could you propose it to the group? What you're developing seems fascinating. Since the possibilities of success will face monumental obstacles, it doesn't seem like a good decision; nonetheless, the challenge stimulates me."

"It's fine with me; let's see what the rest of the partners think."

In the evening, Arthur took a drive to clear his head. He needed to think outside of Konnect's environment. He stopped in a village in front of a bar, the place was busy, and customers dressed with a certain elegance that seemed upscale for the area's rural profile. Once installed, relaxing with a drink, he spotted Nancy Aldrin, the director of the clinic, in the company of a man; Their relationship appeared to be that of a couple.

Arthur approached a waiter.

"Excuse me. I'm going to greet the couple at the table in that corner. I don't remember the gentleman's name, do you know it?" he offered him a twenty-dollar bill.

"It's Mr. Rony Kulmann," he answered as he took the money.

From a distance, Arthur sneakily took a photo of the couple and left the place.

The next morning Arthur consulted with Shivon:

"Tell me objectively, Sis, what is your opinion about the effectiveness of the energy storage chamber to neutralize cancer?"

"It's real. I have no doubt. The effects of chemo are harsh; still, patients have recovered in a shorter time. The supportive therapy Elisa and I practice is also necessary. The word has spread, and during this past month, patients have chosen to avoid traditional chemotherapy; instead, they are willing to try the new alternative therapy. In the last fifteen days, the number of new patients has increased considerably. Why do you ask me?"

"I can't answer you yet; however, I think I have a clue in my investigation."

Arthur entered the laboratory and greeted Ikan.

"How do you feel? Everything fine?" He asked while looking sideways at two assistant scientists.

"Can you come to my office?" Ikan suggested. "Would you like something to drink?"

"Just water, thanks."

"I was waiting for the opportunity to personally thank you for the protection you gave me the other night. I hadn't done it yet because I didn't know you, and I have reasons not to trust easily. Now I think I can give you information which may be helpful in your inquiries."

"Sure, Ikan, I appreciate your sincerity."

"As you know, I'm very advanced in investigating the transmission of wireless electric current. I began this research in secret using resources from the power plant I worked for until a few months ago. Somehow they discovered the experiments I was doing, and they ordered me to suspend them in the form of a threat. Science is my passion. I persisted in working at night on my research. One day I was attacked by unknown subjects and was about to lose my life had it not been for security guards scaring away my attackers. In the anonymity of this place, I felt safe to continue with my experiments; still, I think you're right to suspect there could be a spy who betrayed my whereabouts."

"Don't worry, Ikan, I appreciate the information you just gave me. Now I'd ask you to resist your scientific passion and do nothing new. I just need a little time."

Arthur reflected on the information he had collected. However, the attack's motive was related to two possibilities; the first referring to alternative therapy and the second concerning wireless current. He concluded that the alternative treatment had been public, while wireless power had been under wraps; therefore, his research should focus on alternative therapy for the time.

The photo of Nancy and Rony he took at the bar didn't match a criminal record of either; however, there was something suspicious in the personal data of Roni Kulmann. He was a wealthy individual marketer of drugs used for chemotherapy. By his relationship with Nancy Aldrin as director of the Oncology clinic, Arthur knew what his next move was.

In the middle of the night, Arthur sneaked into Nancy's office. He reviewed the medical records of the patients. He noticed the treatments in most cases used the medications Rony represented. It made no sense to him that the Metropolitan Hospital could have some interest in favoring Rony commercially, so his attention shifted to the accounting records.

According to his suspicion, he discovered two different sets of accounting records: Nancy's own and the one to be reported to the Metropolitan Hospital with false numbers. Nancy and Rony had been making a fortune in chemotherapy treatments, and Ikan's alternative therapy had been rapidly waning their business. Arthur saved a copy of the critical information on a flash drive and left the place.

In an extraordinary meeting, Arthur rendered the report of his investigation to the group. There was astonishment in each of its members' faces except for Elisa, who rarely altered her serene expression. Arthur remembered a famouse phrase she had mentioned two days earlier:

The Mishaps You Experience Test Your Concept of Immortality.

"Congratulations, Arthur," Ariana commented.

Ikan somewhat exalted, "We have the evidence! We can prosecute them!"

"We can't," Arthur intervened. "The evidence I obtained doesn't conform to the legal procedure; it would be inadmissible in court."

"You mean that criminals can get away with it simply because we obtained the evidence with procedural failures?" Ikan set his palms down flat on the table.

"That's right," Arthur said. " An investigation in their offices has to be done by a qualified law officer. It requires a search warrant. I had unauthorized access to their accounting records by evading the system passwords and by entering their property in the middle of the night I incurred in a house raid.

"We need to turn the case over to the police and let them do their job; I have the right contact in mind, I've known him for many years, and he's highly qualified."

"Are you sure the authorities would solve this case?" Ariana asked.

"Definitely."

"I think Arthur is right," Elisa stated. "We must continue with our work focusing on progress and expansion, without condemning anything or anyone. Remember the Chinese proverb: *"It is better to light a candle than curse the darkness."*"

One afternoon Ikan was sitting pensively in a quiet corner of the garden; Shivon walked near him.

"Do I interrupt?"

"You don't; I'm just taking a break.

"May I ask what's in your mind?"

"The truth is I've been working very focused on the transmission of wireless current, and despite my effort to concentrate on the subject, there's an issue that assails my thinking and demands attention from me."

"Do you know what it is?"

"It is related to alternative therapy. I have a modality in mind that would allow us to increase the number of patients treated simultaneously. I have the concept, yet there's a missing link I still need to figure out to be able to define it."

"If you had the chance to grab an opportunity you missed, what would it be?"

Ikan answered without hesitation: "I'd return in time to Bali, to continue with my research on the energy accumulation chamber."

"You mean your modality on Wilhelm Reich's chamber was born in Bali?"

"Yes, it was."

"I think this could be your answer. If you traveled to the place where you started these experiments, your mental processes would reconnect, and your blockage might open. It's only a suggestion."

Enigmatic and Exceptional

Shivon was right; walking through the populous streets of Ubud, on the island of Bali, had made Ikan feel some nostalgia for old times. He bought some trinkets from street vendors who pestered him. Unexpectedly, the sound of the crowd attenuated as he fixed his eyes on a white-bearded man standing at a corner selling herbal remedies.

"It's Ari, my assistant!" He thought as he walked towards him.

"You look younger, Ari! What is your secret?" He greeted him with a bow.

"Nothing I sell here; happiness is the most important ingredient of health and well-being. What a surprise to see you here after so many years!"

"The last time we met, you left without saying goodbye."

"Due to the unsolicited comment I made, I felt I had crossed an authority boundary, and I felt bad."

"You're wrong, and you didn't offend me at all! On the contrary, you shared your wisdom for which I'm still grateful, and I need you. Would you like to work for me again?"

"I feel honored, and I will do my best not to fail you."

The owner of the premises Ikan had rented as a laboratory years ago had died. His children inherited the property but had no use for it.

During the site's improvements, Ikan informed Ari of his experiences in Konnect; Ari remained thoughtful yet, always attentive.

On an evening during a working session, Ikan explained to Ari the unsolved issue he was seeking to figure out in Bali. Both worked long days by methodizing each step of their experiments and documenting the results.

One day Ari stared at Ikan:

"My buck is sick."

"You've always cured your animals. What is the problem?"

"This one I could not."

"What does the vet say?"

"To put it to sleep."

"What are you going to do?"

"You are going to help me heal it."

"Do you want to put the buck in the chamber? We would have to build a special one."

"It won't be necessary. You are right in your new concept of energy accumulation. Instead of bringing the buck here, we would only bring a sample of its immune system; we would then proceed to enhance the cells in a modified chamber and once trained, we reintroduce them into the animal's system to restore it to normal health."

Ikan's whole face lit up:

"We hadn't defined the mechanics; you're right! It could be the key. If it works, please don't go away again!"

~

Nancy Aldrin was convicted. The Oncology Clinic had a new Director, and the Metropolitan Hospital offered to collaborate with Konnect in everything related to alternative therapy.

Ikan made a surprise return to Canada accompanied by Ari, who was appointed Assistant Scientist in Alternative Therapy.

On the day of Konnect's annual meeting for partners and executives, the whole group attended. Towards the end of the session, Elisa took the floor:

"I don't come with a written report, nor do I bring numbers to show results. You know the way I work, and my suggestions are purely intuitive. I feel that Konnect will soon become a large center of attention. This success will threaten many organizations' economic interests, therefore, I see Konnect as vulnerable to possible attacks. My recommendation would be to establish a subsidiary to serve as a backup. This new center should function at a different geographical point from where we currently are. What about Australia?"

"From a strategic point of view, it seems an excellent idea, if my opinion counts at this level." Arthur pointed out.

"What do you mean at this level?" Ariana asked intrigued.

"I act only as a consultant, not as a partner."

"Forgive my mistake by omission," Ariana clarified, "the members of this group had already agreed to accept you as a partner, and I'd forgotten to let you know. You're a de facto partner at this time if you wish."

"I'm excited about Elisa's proposal," Shivon stated.

"Anyone against it? No one?... I also support the idea." Ariana ended the session.

Having taken the step made Elisa feel satisfied. Most of the time, she had remained an observer during the creation and development of Konnect, just giving some guidelines through Shivon's voice.

Elisa had indeed been a beggar, and for years she lived as a drifter rolling around the world. During such time, she experienced innumerable situations within the human social gears. These situations were instrumental to gradually sensitize her ability to feel compassion and empathy for others' pain and suffering.

Compassion and empathy can only be expressed with love. What we call miracles only occur within the context of love. For this reason, Elisa occasionally surprised people with her insight and the ability to appear ready to help in the right place at the right time.

Interrupted Expression of Love

On an off day, Shivon and Ikan were at their favorite place by the river.

She asked spontaneously:

"If you could do something different from what you're doing right now, what would it be?"

"I wouldn't change anything; I consider it a privilege to be doing what I do here, I'm right now in the right place with the right person, and I don't want it to sound cliché."

"Cliché? Do you think there's something not yet been said? A situation not been mentioned in any way? Even this comment I'm making now has been told countless times. When you and I talk, there's no room for cliché, only sincerity.

"Let me change the question: if you wrote the story of your life, what would be the highlight?"

"The present, the work I develop with the group in Konnect, the time I share with you."

Shivon was surprised by the emotional comment. Without meeting his gaze, she picked lint from his shoulder.

"During your talk to the group in Konnect," Ikan added, "you mentioned you had been lead to introspection by health challenges… at that moment, I remember thinking I'd have liked to meet you as a child I'd have wanted to be your playmate.

"As you can see, destiny has brought us together in an exceptional experience. It's a privilege to offer our service in this non-profit organization to contribute something positive to the world.

"Before I met you, I could've defined myself as an analyst; now, after meeting you, I see myself as a witness of how my life turned into an exciting adventure."

"What prompted you to invite me to come to this river for the first time?" Shivon asked in a soft voice.

"I'll try to answer you," Ikan was visibly self-conscious. "Remember that the left hemisphere of my brain predominates, and it is difficult for me to express myself on these matters openly.

"When I first saw you in bed at this clinic, I knew the death of the little kid had impacted you. You were in shock caused by your empathy towards the child's condition. I appreciated your vulnerability as a quality rather than as a weakness. I thought: this is a person who can be trusted; she's tender, warm; it would be a genuinely fortunate individual who had her as a partner."

BOOM! An explosion interrupted their dialogue.

"The sound came from the clinic!" Ikan exclaimed.

The Oncology Clinic staff was alarmed. The explosion was an unexpected event that interrupted all activities. The employees didn't want to return to their posts for fear of new detonations.

Arthur immediately contacted a team of experts to detect additional explosives in the building; He also called a forensics team to investigate the origin of the explosion to obtain data to be used during a criminal investigation.

"Where was the explosion site?" Ikan asked Arthur.

"In medical equipment storage, most of the inventory consisted of energy concentrating chambers."

"My chambers!" Ikan lamented.

Ariana approached Arthur:

"The director of the Metropolitan Hospital just called me, she's on her way, and I have no explanation…"

"Don't worry, for now, just tell her we have two groups of professionals investigating the incident; the staff is safe, and fortunately, there were no deaths or injuries."

Marion Howard, director of the Metropolitan Hospital, briefly surveyed the explosion scene and asked Ariana to speak with her privately.

Marion had the appearance of an executive who acted with authority and kindness simultaneously, and the woman inspired respect.

"The purpose of my visit is a difficult task for me," Marion began the dialogue. "The introduction of alternative therapy in the hospital I run changed my belief system. The rate of successful treatments was astonishing! It was like a breeze of fresh air. At the same time, it exposed our impotence to cure the sick in countless cases with traditional forms of therapy.

"With the high rate of success, without consulting with Konnect I decided to use the chambers to treat patients with conditions other than cancer. A few days ago, the medical team notified me of successful results in patients with diabetes…" Marion paused. "…The news of the explosion this morning hit me like a bucket of chilly water. Suddenly, I realized the risk I incurred if I disrupted the economic infrastructure on which thousands of people depend. I prefer not to elaborate on the subject. I hope you understand me…"

"Of course," Ariana nodded.

"In summary, I have no option other than to cancel the alternative therapy program; at great risks, big decisions. I ask your cooperation for the good of our organizations, to terminate the lease contract between the Metropolitan Hospital and Konnect to avoid future incidents."

"I agree, Marion; I'll inform my partners. I'm sure they'll have no objection."

"Today, I'll have our patients transferred to the Metropolitan Hospital. Thank you very much for your understanding." Marion reached out to say goodbye.

Arthur was busy following up on reports from professionals about the incident. His cell phone showed a call from an unusual origin: It comes from jail, he thought.

"Who's this?"

"I'm Nancy Aldrin Mr. Robinson, please don't hang up!"

"What can I do for you?"

"I need to speak privately with you; it is important. I know you can make arrangements so that nobody can monitor our conversation."

Arthur thought he should have this conversation; it could relate to the attack on the clinic.

"I'll do my best to see you tomorrow."

The next day Nancy Aldrin and Arthur met in a private cell. Nancy was nervous and somewhat withdrawn; Arthur was skeptical, yet curious about Nancy's talk request.

Nancy started the conversation with a tone of justification:

"I know I'm here serving a conviction for criminal acts, and I'm not credible. Despite this, I need to confess the truth; I have a problem of conscience, and I want to help."

"Go ahead; I listen to you."

"My relationship with Rony Kulmann began when I met him as a successful businessman, with the vision of selling the best products available in the field of chemotherapy.

"As our dealings progressed, Ronny turned into a controlling and greedy individual. I was under pressure to have the clinic displace the suppliers who competed with his products. There came a point when I felt guilty and frightened. The time coincided with the attempt to kidnap Ikan.

"The part I want to reveal is that Rony orchestrated the explosion in the clinic. It was part of a plan to prevent alternative therapy from progressing at an institutional level. I could give you concrete data to arrest Rony; but, he's only a pawn on the chessboard, and there would be reprisals for Konnect. Behind all this, there's an anonymous organization with influence in high circles." Nancy was becoming overwhelmed.

Arthur interfered: "With new evidence to prove you acted intimidated under pressure, it could serve as mitigating circumstances to reopen your case. It would be possible to reduce your sentence considerably."

"I'd have to expose Rony and talk about an invisible organization. Most likely, I wouldn't survive to enjoy my freedom. I prefer to serve my sentence in silence with the relative security I have behind these bars, as long as you discreetly handle what I revealed to you."

"Don't worry; I wouldn't jeopardize your security. I appreciate the information you gave me; it will help us to be alert."

~

The explosives detection personnel had completed their job and had cleared the building to be out of danger.

The Konnect partners met to discuss the situation of the company and the steps to follow.

Ariana started the session:

"I understand the risks of retaliation if we pursue criminal activity; however, I'm outraged to see criminal actions go unpunished. I see a fine line between being cautious or being coward."

Arthur raised his hand.

"As a man, I can say that getting carried away by testosterone can be a source of many mistakes; It would not be cowardly to avoid a fistfight if the opponent were bigger and stronger. It would be smarter to opt for survival and the conservation of physical and mental faculties.

"In our case, the enemy doesn't show their face; it's anonymous. It would be like fighting a ghost, and yet we're visible and vulnerable to any attack."

"I withdraw my statement," Ariana recanted. "I couldn't help expressing my frustration."

"Although I didn't say it, I feel the same way," Arthur admitted.

The rest of the partners remained silent; it was apparent they shared the same degree of frustration.

Elisa broke the silence:

"The attack suffered in the clinic couldn't have been foreseen. It would be impossible to prevent something similar or worse from happening in the future. Our excitement made us think we were contributing to making a better world. The problem is the world isn't ready for such a radical change. There are currently several active states of war in various countries of the planet, genocide events haven't ceased, and the murder rate increases by the day. We hear of hate crimes and religious and racial discrimination. The human race hasn't achieved peace. If these events persist, the world won't be ready for a meaningful change. I suggest reviewing the Konnect's objectives. We'll not stop acting; we need to define how we're going to do it."

"Elisa just expressed it very clearly," Shivon said. "We're not to change anything or anyone. What we can do is to change our approach in Konnect, and in principle, I propose the following:

"The term "Alternative Therapy" implies a replacement for conventional therapy. The economic aspect of the medical industry is not willing to lose ground, nor income. We neither seek to profit from our healing methods nor compete with conventional medicine;I suggest using the term 'Complementary Therapy,' which would be applied in tandem with traditional therapy and thus end potential conflicts."

"Thank you, Shivon; I support your proposal; it seems like an excellent idea," Ariana said.

The rest of the group expressed its approval.

⚬⚬⚬

ACHACK

A Year Ago

Elisa traveled in her jeep through the forests of Lennox, Ontario, in Canada. Per her belief system, she hadn't planned an itinerary. She drove her car, attentive to the next event to cross her path. Her old car had no radio or sound system. She thought the lack of background music favored her to stay in the present moment. At a distance, she distinguished a man who moved his arms in a sign for help. Beside him, there was a woman prostrated on the floor. They appeared to be Native American. Elisa stopped the jeep on the side of the road.

"What's happening?"

"It's my wife!" the man replied, "She's about to have a baby. I need to take her to a midwife!"

Elisa got out of the car and checked the woman: who seemed to be in an advanced childbirth process.

"There's no time to take her to a midwife; we need to act right here. I can help; do you authorize me to proceed?"

"Yes! May your ancestors help!"

Elisa improvised what was necessary to attend the emergency with a first aid kit and bottles of water she had in her car. Half an hour later, the woman hugged her baby, and Elisa suggested taking her to the nearest hospital to finish the procedure with professional care.

The man refused.

"We are Chippewa, hospital not for us, take us to our people, they help us."

"What is your name?" Elisa asked.

"Binesi." He pounded his chest.

Elisa took them in her car, guided by Binesi. They arrived at a Native American community in the forest. She was surprised to see this group not integrated into a reservation. Elisa said goodbye to the couple and watched them leave protected by a group of their people around them. She entered her car again and started it up. Before she could drive off, a group of men blocked Elisa's path. One of them approached her window and informed her that 'Chief Achak' wanted to talk to her. He guided Elisa to the hut of the community leader.

"I've been waiting for you for a long time." A strong older man announced. "My name is Achak. I am the chief of this tribe. I thank you for the help you provided to the Binesi couple; this fact confirms you're the one I've been waiting for."

"Who are you waiting for? How do you know it's me?"

"During a ceremony performed in a sacred ritual, I saw you were coming here with a special mission, not necessarily for my people, all the same, we must help you, it is the will of those who live 'on the other side.'"

"What is the mission I have here?"

"You don't know it yet; however, it originates here. Let me explain:

"Several generations ago, our ancestors discovered some caverns and an elaborate tunnel system in this area. They used caves and tunnels to store groceries, allowing them to survive the winters; they also used them as underground shelters to hide from aggressive tribes. At present, we keep the existence of the caverns secret and only use them to shelter us during the severity of the winters."

"Why do you tell me all this? Who are you? Why do you express yourself in a more structured way than the rest of your people?"

"I am Achak, Chippewa of origin. I managed to be educated outside the reservation by a government program to help my people more effectively. Challenging times are coming.

"I tell you all this because, in my vision, I noticed a new socio-economic order is coming, there will be many conflicts. You're part of the members of the new order and need protection. The flow you intuitively follow brought you here; you're in the right place."

Elisa interrupted the dialogue with her mind; she blocked internal questions to allow her intuition to manifest:

"Some time ago, I mentioned to a young woman how the human drama unfolds through THE MIND OF A THOUSAND FACES; you are one of those characters right now."

"And I was waiting for you," Achak interrupted, "I know what you mean: *The One became many, and the many of us are One.*" He was silent and waited patiently…

"You're right!" Elisa replied. "Somehow, I feel I'm in the right place. Thank you, Achak. My name is Elisa."

In the days that followed, Elisa spoke with members of the tribe to help them with the guidance they requested. Achak ordered them to build a wooden cabin for Elisa at the foot of a cliff. The site of the house had access to the underground system of tunnels and caverns. They had carefully disguised the entrance to a secret passage behind a wall in the cabin.

Ten Years Ago

Shivon and Ariana, as young teenagers, gathered in Ariana's mansion, talked about their next high school graduation party.

Shivon was showing little enthusiasm:

"I'm not sure to attend; it's an event with no meaning for me; my friends are not at this school. In reality, you're my only friend there."

The housekeeper came into the room to report young Arthur had come to pick up his sister Shivon. Both friends went downstairs to meet him.

Arthur awaited with a gift package at his feet.

"Thanks, brother! What did you bring to me?" Shivon giggled, standing on her toes in excitement.

"It's for Ariana," Arthur answered with some shyness.

"For me? What's the occasion?

Upon opening the package, she discovered an Australian Shepherd puppy.

"It's beautiful! I love it! Thanks, Arthur, what a surprise!"

After playing a few moments with the puppy, Shivon offered to take him to the garden to start training it's 'sphincters.'

"You surprised me, Arthur, is there something you want to tell me?"

Arthur remained silent, so she continued:

"I do have something to ask you; Would you come to prom with me?"

"I'd do it, thanks for thinking of me, the case is I won't be here; tomorrow I'll take a plane to join the army, not even Shivon knows. There's this unsustainable family situation…"

"You don't have to explain anything to me; I just would like to keep in touch. Would you let me know how to reach you?"

"You don't know how difficult it is for me to answer your question Ariana, my departure will mean a long absence. I think it would be better to leave our friendship as it is."

All of a sudden, Shivon entered with the puppy. "Did you think of a name yet? Ouch. What's with the faces?"

Present Time

Ikan and Ari, aboard a commercial jet, traveled to Australia. The objective was to find a strategic site to establish a Konnect subsidiary where Ikan could continue his research.

Ikan appeared outraged.

"It seems unfair to hide thousands of miles away just to do things right, to work safely on scientific progress."

Ari half shrugged in his usual measured manner:

"It's the way the human drama develops. Imagine for a moment how insubstantial the plots of all the movies you've seen would be if you took away the elements of corruption, revenge, intrigue, sabotage, chaos, and violence."

"I understand your argument Ari, you're right; regardless, I remain indignant. I'm going to sleep now; we have a long flight ahead."

~

Konnect had gradually changed its profile. The place functioned as a meditation, yoga center and offered wellness programs through physical, mental, and emotional support. Physical Therapy included acupuncture, hypnotherapy, and energy storage chambers as a supportive treatment for traditional medicine.

Arthur was in Robinson's offices. His private phone announced a particular call.

"Arthur? I'm Ariana."

"Everything fine?"

"Yes, all right, I haven't seen you here for three days."

"There are matters I need to attend; my father has health issues..."

"I understand, Arthur; I just wanted to know how you were. I hope everything goes well; please let me know if I can help."

"Thanks, Ariana, see you soon."

It didn't take long for Arthur to enter Ariana's office.

"Regarding your call this morning, tell me what's going on."

"Everything's fine. Konnect running smoothly, we have no disasters to deal with."

"I know you, Ariana, there's something you're not telling me." Arthur insisted.

She lowered her head:

"This morning, a weight oppressed my heart; I was low-spirited. My nanny called me from my house to inform me they had to put Tyson to sleep. Do you remember the puppy you gave me? It was ten years old. It was too sick, and there was no other choice.

"You've no idea how important your gift was for me. You gave me the embodiment of qualities humans often lack; unconditional love, for example. Tyson didn't care if I had money, whether I was pretty or not, some days, I ignored him for being busy, and despite everything, the faithful furball always showed his unconditional love. Tyson could perceive my emotions and suffered when I didn't feel well. It was always willing to play. Its main goal was to make me happy." Ariana was beginning to break.

Arthur realized Ariana had unconsciously referred to the company the dog provided her, unlike him, who had moved away from her life. Mixed feelings invaded him inside.

He had always maintained a special affection for Ariana; only the family conflict with his father and the post-traumatic effects of war had affected his ability to keep a stable, affectionate relationship. On the other hand, his performance in Konnect had given him reassurance. Somehow it had served to dispel the few ghosts left in the closet.

Arthur placed his hand on Ariana's shoulder:

"I propose you to request Tyson's body be cremated, and together you and I will spread its ashes in the most meaningful place where you shared happy days."

In a hotel in Brisbane, Australia, Ikan explained in detail the purpose of this trip to Ari:

"The world is about to experience significant socioeconomic changes. Economic power will shift to China, India, Indonesia, and possibly Australia. It isn't only the financial part that's relevant to me. It is crucial to find a place that offers political stability and respect for human rights; however, I need to cover my scientific objective, above all. Let me explain:

"Our planet is a giant electric generator like any motor with positive and negative poles rotating on an axis to produce constant energy. I'm convinced ancient civilizations not recorded in history used this energy to illuminate their homes, power their vehicles, in the construction of their structures, in short, for everything that required the use of energy.

"Some pyramids remain as vestiges of some cultures somehow using this 'free energy network 'around the planet. The pyramid itself wasn't the only critical element concerning the generation of energy, but also its location. It is essential to determine a specific site within the 'energy network' which naturally exists in the globe, to establish our research laboratory."

Ikan ended his explanation and observed how Ari remained immutable as if he were oblivious to the subject.

After a few moments, Ari replied:

"I understand what you are looking for: it refers to the meridians through which the energy of our world circulates. In Indonesia, we use them for therapeutic purposes, agriculture, and meditation; yet, those are only secondary meridians. The application you need requires the main meridians; one of the most important circulates in the northern hemisphere, and it's aligned with the pyramids of Egypt, except a laboratory could not be established in that area."

"What do you suggest?" Ikan asked.

"If we take into account the socio-economic considerations, the ideal place would be Cambodia, since the meridian passes right through the Angcar site, and the laboratory could be established somewhere nearby."

A burst of joy warmed Ikan from within; he held Ari by his shoulders:

"Ari, you've no idea how much I appreciate your insight in solving the problems presented to us; I feel I haven't given you anything, and yet you've contributed so much to me!"

"On the contrary, I am the one who has to thank you for giving me a purpose."

Atonement

Elisa and Shivon conducted a guided meditation session for a group of students. Arthur peeked in from the enclosure entrance and, with a sign of his hand, caught Shivon's attention. She silently made Elisa understand she needed to leave the room to answer her brother's call.

"Sorry for the interruption Sis, it's an emergency with dad."

"What's going on?"

"For the past three years, he's refused to have routine medical checkups. Two days ago, he was diagnosed with an inoperable brain tumor which is causing multiple organ failure. Doctors say he won't last the day. He's very distraught and asks to see you. He apologizes for not being able to come."

"Let's go!" She stomped her foot.

Edward Robinson was in the intensive care unit being monitored with all imaginable medical devices.

"Thank you for coming, daughter."

Daughter? It's the first time in twenty-five years she refers to me this way, she thinks.

"Don't get agitated, Dad, give me your hand, and we'll talk."

With effort, Edward spoke:

"I was dominant and proud by cutting you out of my life, and later, when I realized my mistake, I was a coward by not apologizing. What can I do so you don't hate me?"

"Of course, I don't hate you, Dad, and there's nothing to forgive. Forget about any feelings of guilt you might have since you didn't hurt me. The past no longer exists, now let's talk about what you want in the present."

"The Robinson business consortium is in your hands along with your brother Arthur. It will be in you to restructure the Robinson Companies in a professional, ethical manner. Our cruises have been the scene of criminal acts: passengers missing at sea, raped women.

"In the area of artificial intelligence, they've used software to get easy money from casino customers; they've also invaded the public's privacy to make them more consumerist.

"In the last six months, I canceled a multitude of customer contracts from our companies, which in my opinion were making dishonest use of our products and services."

"Okay, Dad, I understand you, and I agree, don't get tired!"

"My end is here. When the lights go out, I'm going to be 'nothing' as if I never existed!" Edward expressed his anguish, and the sound of the monitoring system indicated a fast pulse.

Shivon gathered her strength and spoke to him tenderly:

"Dad, listen to me closely; I'm going to ask you a favor. I know it won't be easy for you. Please listen to me for five minutes with all your attention and very important, without interrupting me. I promise you it is not about hypnosis, meditation, or any of those modalities you've always rejected. I only ask for your attention. Do you agree?

Edward accepted.

"Close your eyes and just listen to my words. I need you to be calm and this time to be just for you and me, for us.

"Now I want you to go back to your childhood... when you were about ten years old or so and remember a scene that comes to your mind... whatever it may be, it doesn't need to be something significant, just an image that comes to your mind... who is with you? What is happening?... watch it in detail.

"Now leave the scene and go to a time in your life when you were about thirty years old... take your time... where are you?... who are you with?... observe the scene well... look at the details...

"Well, now slowly open your eyes and continue listening to me:

"You brought to your memory two scenes: the child and the young man's. The boy was a temporary character who changed over time. The young man was another temporary character who also changed over time; however, there was a spectator in both scenes, someone watching. You just experienced it! *The observer is who you are.* The child you observed no longer exists; neither does the young man. *The observer saw the two scenes and is aware it exists; it does not change, and it is immortal. That is your true being; it is who you are.* There's nothing to fear!"

Edward looked into Shivon's eyes and smiled, then a persistent alarm indicated the monitoring system warning; Edward's vital signs were on a flat line, and his stormy life had in conclusion ended with an expression of peace.

The sixth sense,
the sense of "knowing",
is the compass needle
that points us
in the right direction.

The Birch Agreement

In a secluded place away from the busy areas in the Konnect complex, there was a spot known as 'The Birch.' This site was unique for the peace experienced under the leafy tree.

Elisa invited the group members—including Ari—to listen to a talk labeled 'The Birch Agreement.' Once all of them seated comfortably, Elisa started her speech:

"Difficult times are predicted due to climatic changes. Instability in the economy, racial, religious, and foreign policy tensions will compound the crisis. It is not my intention to talk about calamities. There's not much we can do to avoid difficulties; however, we can control how we react to adversity and the type of experience we will have.

"The concepts I'm going to deal with are not new; you've undoubtedly read about the subject or heard them mentioned in some way. I invite you to make suggestions so that, as a group, we try to be on the same page.

"This moment is only for us... let's put on hold all notifications and reminders.

"During our daily activity, sometimes problems overwhelm us, and we forget the potential power we have to solve them. In our Inner Being, we have infinite power to:

Organize.
Establish correlation —of people, opportunities, events.
Be creative.
To know WE ARE all we need.

"The key is to establish contact with those abilities, and this key is the awareness of my Inner Being, who I really AM.

"It is not necessary to solve problems rationally. Our Inner Being is waiting for an opportunity to manifest, to guide us!

"On many occasions, I've been asked how to establish contact with our Inner Being. The way can vary according to the person and the circumstances; it is essential to perceive beyond the five senses and reach the sixth sense. Our senses are sight, hearing, smell, taste, and touch. The sixth sense is that of knowing, which remains latent until we activate it.

"The contact with our Inner Being always occurs in the present moment; the past doesn't matter; it requires some form of meditation:

> *Silence, stillness.*
> *Stop analyzing and evaluating. Stop dialogue with the mind.*
> *Contact with nature.*
> *Depending on the circumstances, you can practice:*
> *meditative walks, guided meditations, drawing a mandala.*

"The goal is to stop 'doing' and start 'being.' Doing is a function of the physical body while "being" is a function of the soul.

"Now, why is it so important to reach the state of 'being'? This state is the moment in which we contact our Inner Essence; it is the origin of all possibilities. At this moment, we create the circumstances to manifest our intention—a specific thought—in the reality of the physical world.

"Active meditation increases our awareness. We express ourselves with more clarity, increase our self-confidence, free ourselves from fear; we manifest more creativity, feel happy without apparent cause, and our life synchronizes positively.

"In our social structure, there's a generally accepted concept:

If you don't have, you are not.

"The truth is: *If you really ARE you will always have what you need.*

"This is a summary of the concepts I use during the classes I teach to my students. I'm receptive to any comments or suggestions you might like to make to improve my explanations."

Arthur raised his hand:

"The only thing I can say is I have a great deal to learn, and I'm going to attend to your classes."

"Me too," Ariana confirmed.

Ari smiled and nodded. What was he thinking?

FALLEN ANGELS

"I received an invitation for two this morning," Ikan commented to Shivon as they strolled together in Konnect's garden. "It is a reception to award the prize of the year in science. Would you like to attend?"

"As far as I know, you're not a member of the association. Do you have any idea who sent you the invitation?"

"I don't know."

"You keep your work completely off the radar; so far, you've tried to be invisible in the scientific world. There's something I don't like. I distrust the invitation. I'd ignore it."

Ikan reflected on Shivon's arguments:

"You're right. Why would they invite someone unrelated to the association? I'm not a member of any social club. I don't have credit cards, nor I use any social media. How did they manage to find me?"

"Are you telling me you want to go?"

"Blame it on my sentimental side. The incongruity of this, is that I feel a little nostalgic about the scientific community with which I never had ties."

"I don't want to sound alarmist Ikan, except the idea smells fishy. I wouldn't want to go against my instinct."

"I respect your feeling Shivon; I'll go by myself for a brief time just out of curiosity."

Ikan blended in the crowd, watched the scene without alternating with the attendees. Listened to the host recite the praise for the winner, the music, the applause, the award...

At the end of the ceremony, he realized the nostalgia he experienced earlier belonged to an Ikan who had changed. Public approval was no longer an incentive for his work. He had accomplished the objective of his attendance at the ceremony.

Ikan decided to retire and walked through the solitary parking lot.

A truck approached quickly, braked abruptly next to him, and two individuals held him, covered his head with a hood, and injected him with a substance that made him lose consciousness.

~

Shivon went to Elisa's room:

"Elisa, wake up."

"What's going on?"

"I know it's too late, excuse me, I'm worried. Ikan went to an event that has long been over and hasn't called me; he doesn't answer his phone. I have a bad feeling."

Elisa breathed deeply several times.

"In case it makes you feel better, I can tell you I perceive Ikan alive and without physical pain... he's moving away, they're taking him somewhere against his will... he's probably being kidnapped..."

"What do we do? Notify the police? Shivon asked.

"Let's check with Arthur first; he has experience in these situations."

∼

Ikan remained in a lethargic state for several hours; in his state of drowsiness, he vaguely perceived voices in a language not entirely unknown to him while he could hear a constant sound of an airplane engine, and then, nothing, again unconsciousness.

∼

Arthur reflected on the information Shivon provided regarding the situation with Ikan.

"At this level, I think we should wait for the captors, if there are any, to let us know their intentions. We need to know what they want."

"Wait? how long?"

"About seventy-two hours. Meanwhile, I'm going to alert my group of Sharks."

"What do you mean by your group of Sharks?"

"It's something I've never told you. Sometime after I departed from the army, it was difficult for me to integrate into civilian life. Being out of action and missions made me feel purposeless. With the financial resources we have in the Robinson consortium, I gradually recruited a select group of former members of the special forces to act on our own in emergency cases. I know we function outside the legal framework. As you know, the slowness and complexity of bureaucracy sometimes favor criminals. I can say we've helped several families in some cases, and that made me feel better."

"Take care of it, brother; you know this aspect of life better than I do."

~

Ikan gradually regained consciousness. He was in a closed, white room, like a hospital, a big screen in front of him. He got up, took a few steps around the room, and saw a doorbell next to a closed-door; he pressed it a couple of times and waited.

The screen turned on, and the image of a digitally altered face appeared.

"Welcome, Mr. Stolls."

"Who are you? What am I doing here?"

"For your safety, I can't tell you who I am. We'll talk when necessary through this screen. I apologize for making you come against your will. The fact is, circumstances press on us, and we need your services. I assure you we're not ungrateful; if you comply with what we request, we'll take you back to your home, and we'll reward you generously."

"What happens if I don't fulfill what you require of me?"

"At the moment, we're not going to talk about it since we trust you're a reasonable man. Now you're going to meet Raam, who will give you instructions. I welcome you again. My identity is Kroll."

The screen went out. A few minutes later, the door opened, and a young man came in, tall, with a beard, dressed in Indonesian fashion.

"I'm Raam, follow me."

Ikan slid him a guarded look, then both walked down a corridor and entered a large laboratory with high-tech equipment.

Raam led Ikan to a private office and asked him to take a seat.

"In this place, we don't have much contact with the outside world. You have a private sleeping room, you'll have clothing, food and you can make a list of personal needs. We spend most of our time in this laboratory and in an enclosed garden attached to this building."

"Are you here also as a prisoner?" Ikan inquired.

"Don't interrupt me!" Raam admonished, "Pay attention:

I'm going to give you an individual's DNA sample. It would help if you created a genetically engineered virus to attack that person and no one else. It is imperative that the virus only attacks the target I'm going to give you."

"Are you ordering me to kill someone?"

"I'm not. I'm instructing you that the objective is to have the subject temporarily out of function. You've access to the entire laboratory. Let me know anything you need."

~

Elisa took in a deep, long breath; she rubbed her temples and closed her eyes. She tried to keep Shivon calm by giving her emotional support:

"I continue to perceive Ikan alive; he's not physically injured…I see two islands connected by a bridge… Ikan is on the big island…"

"Do you have any idea where those islands are?" Shivon asked in a quiet voice, trying not to interrupt Elisa's trance.

"No… I only see a tropical environment… and nothing else for the moment."

~

Ikan had a moral conflict with the task imposed on him. He tried to figure out how to temporarily incapacitate the person without irreversible damage and thus fulfill the objective. Causing permanent damage would be relatively straightforward; however, a temporary disability represented an overly complicated challenge.

The next day Ikan approached Raam:

"*Saya Berbicara Bahasa Indonesian*", (I speak Indonesian).

"It isn't allowed to speak Indonesian in this laboratory," Raam retorted."What do you want?"

"Could you assign me an exclusive cubicle for my work?" Ikan requested.

Hours later, Ikan walked through the garden, and Raam tackled him.

"If you're a spy, don't waste your time with me; I'm part of the team in this place."

"I understand." Ikan replied, "I want to make it clear I'm not a spy."

"You speak Indonesian with an accent; where did you learn it?" Raam inquired.

"I had a laboratory in Ubud on the island of Bali; my assistant taught me the language. I developed a friendship with him, and Indonesian helped me to have better communication. His name was Ari; I asked him his last name; he indicated that they don't use last names in Bali; however, sometimes they added 'Wayan' to their name to differentiate themselves."

Raam muted with Ikan's information and changed the topic of the conversation:

"How are you doing with your project?"

"I'm sorting data; I need my watch. Could you give it back to me? I'm an organized individual; I use it to take my medications, and even to regulate my circadian rhythms. I know it sounds silly, I could wear any watch; however, I've used mine for many years; even if it seems absurd, it is part of my comfort zone."

"I'll see what I can do." Raam turned and left.

~

Arthur had contacted several Shark group members and informed them of the limited information he had about the case. The team remained on call, ready to act on short notice.

~

Ikan had his watch again and discreetly operated a combination of buttons, the numbers: -8.7333   115.5333 appeared on the cover.

Since Ikan investigated the 'meridians' through which the planet's energy circulates, he had programmed a feature on his watch to display his earthly location by geographical coordinates. Now he knew where he was!

Again, Raam approached Ikan as they walked on the garden:

"Ari, your assistant, did you ever notice if he had a tattoo on his forearm?"

"Yes, he had a tiger; he told me it was a family symbol."

"Did his tattoo looked like this? Raam discovered his forearm and revealed an image of the tiger."

"Yes, identical to this one."

"I think I know who he is," Raam affirmed. Can you tell me where he is?

"He works with me in Canada."

"His health, how is it?"

"Excellent, the last time I saw him, it was excellent."

"I'm going to confide you that Ari is my father. I was born because of a relationship he had with my mother, named Indah. My family didn't allow my mother to marry Ari because he's of a lower caste.

"When I was a child, Ari visited me surreptitiously, and he began to stimulate my inclination for science. Because of our affinity, I felt the need to apply the tiger tattoo on my arm one day. From that moment, the relationship with my father was blocked by my family group, and since then, I lost contact with him."

"Why do you trust me with all this information?" Ikan asked.

"I don't know; I hope it's not a mistake on my part."

"May I ask you again if you're here by your will?" Ikan inquired in a confident tone.

"Initially, yes. It unnerved me how my father was discriminated against for being a seller of medicinal herbs on the street. I didn't want to suffer the same fate. This organization contacted me because I specialize in molecular biology and software management at a proficient level."

Ikan went back to his question:

"When I asked you if you were here of your own free will, what did you mean 'initially yes.'"

"The work assigned to me, in the beginning, was aimed at improving the yield of rice crops. Later they gave me considerable monetary loans to meet the medical needs of members of my family. Some time ago, they asked me to develop genetically engineered plants with psychoactive properties. This type can produce drugs with a strong stimulus, susceptible to a high degree of addiction. Of course, I don't want to do it, though at this level, I'm committed and trapped."

"What is the purpose of the virus I was requested?"

"I don't know where they intend to start the plantations; I just know the president of the country would not allow it. As soon as your virus acts, they have a successor president ready to act as a savior of the impaired patient's situation. Once installed in power, the substitute president will control the situation in favor of the plantations."

"I appreciate the risk you took by giving me all this information; I'll correspond by taking the risk of confessing something to you":

Ikan took a flash drive out of his pocket.

"This unit contains the programming necessary to send a message indicating the coordinates of my location. The local system's filters would not detect anything suspicious in the message content since it doesn't contain any Latin characters. Should I give it to you?"

"We don't have access to the internet in our laboratory computers; all the same, I'll find a way." Raam took the flash drive and walked away.

~

Shivon was in meditation. Her phone notified of a new message. She usually ignored the notifications while in meditation; however, this time something told her she had to attend to it. She checked the text:

Ικαν -8.7333 115.5333.

Ahh, digital garbage! she thought; she was about to erase it, but a sensation in her plexus prevented it. She looked at the numbers and reflected: *They seem to have an order; apparently, they're not digital garbage.* She went to her brother Arthur, who was about to get in his car.

Upon reading the text, Arthur reacted immediately:

"It's a message from Ikan Sis! His name is in Greek characters, and the numbers represent the coordinates of his location!"

The group met immediately at Ariana's office, and checked the coordinates on the computer:

"These are the islands of Nusa Lembongan and Nusa Penida," Ariana affirmed.

"Ari, do you know the place?" Shivon asked.

"Yes, I was there at some time."

"How do you cross from one island to another?"

"A bridge connects them," Ari confirmed.

Shivon looked at Elisa, giving her credit for the accuracy she had during her vision.

"If you allow me, I would like to join you to rescue Ikan," Ari pleaded to Arthur: "I owe him fidelity; it is part of my cultural upbringing. Also, I know the island, and I have an idea where he could be."

Elisa approached Ari with discretion and in a faint voice:

"On the big island at a point near the sea, there are two natural rock towers; that's the place!"

Elisa watched Ari as he left the room and pondered: "He is an embodiment of wisdom, yet, he acts devoid of vanity. Ikan is fortunate to have such an assistant."

Raam showed up at the teleconference room in response to a call from Kroll.

Kroll appeared on the screen.

"We haven't heard from you Raam, your term expired. Something new?"

"Despite I haven't made germination periods grow faster, I'm still on track. In the meantime, I've prepared some samples of a low-cost chemical drug that can be produced with minimal equipment, anywhere, and has no lethal effects. Your customers could be repetitive and long-lasting."

"Sounds interesting. Does the stimulus compare to the genetically modified psychoactive plant?"

"No, the stimulus is not as strong, still first-rate. We can produce the drug immediately to generate income while concluding with my experimentation."

"This time, we're going to take your initiative into account, and we extend the deadline for another week, don't let us down!"

The screen turned off.

Raam walked by Ikan's desk and left him a message on a card: "I'll see you in the garden in 10 minutes"

"It is necessary to be careful with what we say in the laboratory; I suspect we're being monitored," Raam warned.

"I agree; I have also thought about it from the beginning."

"I need to talk to you about something that has been bothering me," Raam confided:

"Kroll has been pressuring me to produce the genetically engineered plants with psychoactive properties; the deadline ended, and as a last resort to buy time, I offered to provide him with samples of a chemical drug, which I can produce temporarily. He accepted, and gave me another week, yet I'm worried."

"Are you concerned about the damage your drug is going to cause?"

"No, although the drug has a certain psychotropic effect, I consider it a lesser evil for addicts since it doesn't have lethal effects in the event of an overdose, nor does it produce addiction; Of course, this isn't known by Kroll. What I want to tell you is: I had to choose the least of the evils to survive the moment; however, I still feel bad about what I do."

"You've acted right under the circumstances," Ikan stated. Since you managed to send my message, it is very likely we could've help soon. I suggest we actively work on these projects we're not going to finish."

The Sharks' group traveled at night in an Incat Crowther Catamaran with high-tech equipment and a helicopter onboard. They navigated near their destination and gathered to review their action plan. Ari asked to make some comments:

"The small island receives visitors all year round, so it would not be a likely place to establish the type of facilities of our search. The main island has rugged terrain; it is not suitable for tourism; therefore, it is more private. I don't think it is necessary to explore the whole island, since the most usable part for industrial development is northwest. I know the island well because, in past years, I collected unique medicinal plants in this locality.

"You mentioned the surprise factor for an assault. I suggest you allow me to explore the area on foot, posing as a plant collector, which I have always done. As soon as I discover the location of the facilities, I will leave a tracking device hidden on the site and return to the ship."

The men had remained silent, attentively listening to Ari's suggestions.

Arthur exclaimed excited:

"Ari, I didn't know your strategist side; you do very well! I approve of your plan!"

In the early morning of the next day, Ari's figure sneaked through the island's northwest area near the sea. He discovered two natural rock towers; still, he didn't see any type of construction. He examined around and only saw weeds. He couldn't resist the temptation to collect a Jelisa Turmeric specimen and put it in his bag. Without warning, two individuals surprised him from behind and took him prisoner. One of the attackers triggered a concealed button on one of the towers, and a door opened. Ari pressed his bag and activated the tracking device, which was hiding among the herbs. One of the attackers snatched his sack and threw it on the ground before entering the door.

Ari was guided inside the complex and taken to the teleconference room.

The screen turned on, and Kroll appeared:

"Who do we have here? A visitor?"

Ari was silent.

"Who are you? What are you doing on my property?"

"I don't know what your property is; I'm just looking for medicinal plants."

"Your visit is timely; you'll provide us with a service. Let Raam come!" Kroll ordered.

Raam entered the room and couldn't prevent his expression of surprise upon seeing Ari, his father.

Ari remained immutable.

Kroll watched the scene:

"What's the matter, Raam? Do you know him?"

His expression softened.

"Ahh, you were surprised to see one of your kind," Kroll said. "I'm going to ask you for a loyalty test; I need you to use our visitor— What's your name?"

"Ari."

"I need you to use Ari to prove how an overdose of the drug you propose isn't lethal. You only have one hour."

Click, the screen turned off.

Raam took Ari silently to the garden, who informed with caution:

"I'm not alone; we must act quickly; it is necessary to light a fire as if it were a ceremonial act. Where's Ikan? He must join us!"

Raam brought a briefcase with chemicals and proceeded to improvise a ceremonial fire. Ari threw in some plants, which began to produce smoke.

Ikan quickly joined them in the garden while Ari, with discretion, signaled him not to act surprised.

The sound of a helicopter's engine invaded the area. The aircraft approached the garden flying at low altitudes. It fired missiles towards the laboratory door producing several explosions. Some guards began firing at the helicopter parapeted behind the smoking walls. The aircraft launched more missiles to cover its landing. Ari, Ikan, and Raam proceeded to go onboard. Arthur prevented Raam's access for not knowing him, and a bullet suddenly hit him on his back. Ari descended from the aircraft to assist him; Ikan yelled as loud as he could at Arthur: "HE'S WITH US! HE'S ARI'S SON!" Arthur reacted and helped father and son to get on the chopper, which rose at high speed, disappearing for good into the distance.

Arthur checked Raam's wound:

"There seems to be no damage to any organ, or artery. 'The Bone breaker 'will attend you on the ship."

Ikan, baffled, looked at Arthur.

"'The Bone breaker' is our surgeon on board," Arthur clarified.

~

Elisa, Ariana, and Shivon celebrated Ikan's rescue mission success.

"Did you know Ari is coming back bringing a son?" Ariana commented intrigued. "His name is Raam. Arthur didn't give me more details. The news from the members of our group never ceases to amaze me. Arthur informed me their return trip would take a few more days due to an injury Raam suffered during the rescue, and required surgery onboard the ship."

"I miss my colleagues," Shivon yearned. "I feel as if Konnect suffered from anemia. No offense intended for those present."

"Once we're together, we'll operate at full steam." Ariana asserted.

"Your wish will be granted beyond your imagination," Elisa pointed out. "I don't mean to sound alarmist; nonetheless, there's something I'd like to mention n just between the three of us; not in a board meeting.

"There's a situation the governments and the media don't report with accuracy. The problem is related to global warming. It starts with the water:

"As the temperature rises in the world, the snow in the mountains decreases or, in some cases, disappears. As a result, the rivers' collected water is not enough to irrigate the crops; the agriculture industry suffers. The desert areas of the planet have grown in extension. Given the increasing global overpopulation, there are millions of people who are already suffering from hunger. The shortage of water and food increases criminal activity. There's an exodus of millions of refugees fleeing to countries with better climate, as those closer to the extremes of the hemispheres, such as Canada, northern Europe, and Russia. All these movements involve riots, looting, and the inability of the rulers to control the chaos. This prospect is happening in the not too distant future, and the first symptoms are beginning to manifest in the form of wars, illegal trafficking, inflation, political and social unrest. In short, you already know what I'm talking about."

Ariana had been listening intently, then asked: "In our present, here and now, do you see an immediate risk?"

"As I mentioned before, beyond what you could imagine. Buckle up your seat belts because we're about to take off!"

Light and Shadow

Two weeks later, Arthur and the rest of the group traveled by plane back home. As they flew over the Ontario area, they saw public disturbances and crowds moving toward the northwest area of Lake Ontario.

"Our area is in danger!" Arthur exclaimed, "We have to land as soon as possible!"

The authorities had notified Konnect of the impending invasion. They had urged them to evacuate the place.

Arthur and his group arrived at Konnect.

"We have to go back to the plane together! We landed half an hour from here."

Konnect members took only the essential items they could carry and got ready to leave.

An employee of the hangar told Arthur that the mob had arrived and seized the plane.

Elisa raised her voice:

"Please listen to me! We need to go to my cabin; we'll be safe there!"

"Your cabin? Why should we go to your cabin in these circumstances?" Ikan questioned her.

"There's no time to explain; there's something you don't know. Please trust me; we'll be safe there!"

Everyone departed in two vehicles headed to the cabin. Upon approaching the area, Elisa instructed them to leave the trucks on the road away from the house.

Once inside the hut, Elisa briefly informed the group about the existence of the tunnels and caverns. She then proceeded to open the secret access to the tunnel and, one by one, the group members entered into the unknown.

"Why is there lighting in this tunnel? Where does it lead?" Arthur asked.

"I've never explored it," Elisa admitted. "I understand it reaches an outside exit about a mile away in a remote area in the mountains. The Chippewa assured me we would be safe."

At some point, the tunnel connected with a cave of exceptional beauty. The site was broad and high, with stalactites and stalagmites interspersed with selenite crystals.

"This is a good place for an older woman like me to take a break." Elisa declared.

"It looks like a glass cathedral!" Ariana commented.

"They're giant gypsum crystals," Ikan explained. "As I see them, their size ranges from three to twelve feet in length. We're looking at a process that took Nature from five hundred thousand to nine hundred thousand years to build, depending on each piece's dimensions. What puzzles me," he added, examining the walls, "is that this place is lit by wireless electricity. I wonder: Who does it belong to?"

The group resumed their walk, and at the end of the tunnel, they noticed what appeared to be outdoor light.

As they approached the illuminated area, they noticed the cavern expanded into a massive cavity in the mountain, with natural light from the outside. The panoramic view revealed a majestic cliff of considerable height. In the gigantic cave, they observed architectural structures with human activity moving in various directions.

A group of four light-colored uniformed individuals greeted them in a friendly tone:

"Can you identify yourselves?" one of them requested.

"Achak sends us," Elisa reported.

"Welcome to Xonnel; please follow us."

The group stepped into a modern structure. They walked through its interior, which showed impeccable cleanliness. In a sedative colored room, the group settled around a conference table.

In a few moments, a middle-aged man showed up with the appearance of a laboratory scientist.

"Welcome, my name is Karel; I'm in charge of Xonnel. I'm highly interested in getting to know you in as much detail as possible. I suggest you settle in temporary rooms and when ready we'll get to know each other. I'll explain to you who we are and what we do here."

The group members exchanged their impressions upon their arrival in one of their assigned rooms.

"I have a positive feeling about Karel," Elisa affirmed. "I suggest that we act openly and provide him with information about who we are and what we do. I perceive this place offering exciting opportunities."

For several days, the specialized staff of Xonnel interviewed each of the newcomers. Once the interviews concluded, Karel invited them to a meeting.

"I want to thank you for your honesty and willingness to inform Xonnel about your profile and abilities. I infer that fate brought you together, and you've become a closely knit group; I will respect your team unity as such, for as long as you decide. I want to propose your collaboration in a series of functions, projects, and research areas. Your qualifications are valuable to us. Xonnel is a unique community devoted to preserve and improve the quality of life in our world. There's a higher-order above governments, the oil industry, pharmaceutical laboratories, and the Federal Reserve. Thanks to this higher-order, Xonnel has an independent existence, as do other organizations that act incognito in various parts of the world. Some have partially come to the public eye like CERN on the border of France and Switzerland; and area 51 in Nevada USA.

"As you're aware, there is a commotion taking place in the world. There will be less and less time to study and research. People will focus on survival. After some time, when the crisis is over, the planet will regain its balance.

"Our job is to work to safeguard knowledge and be prepared to support the new era.

"If any of you wishes to return to the outside world, you can do it at any time; this isn't a prison. Those of us who live here have experienced happiness and satisfaction. In my case, I was born here. However, sometimes in my life, I've made short trips to other countries for scientific purposes.

"From this moment, you're free to move about and interact with the inhabitants of Xonnel.

"I'll make individual appointments with each one of you to discuss possible positions to be filled and projects to develop."

∼

After a few days, Arthur and Ariana exchanged their impressions:

" If you had to choose living here or returning to the outside world in its current circumstances, what have you thought after weighing the pros and cons?" Arthur asked.

"My life was taking a very stimulating course in the outside world, yet I assure you the environment I was interested in has already changed; from now on, the circumstances will be less and less desirable. Karel offered me a prominent position to organize Xonnel projects in all their complexity, which excites me.

"To answer your question, I'm inclined to try a new life here. What about you?"

"For his knowledge in molecular biology and software programming, my work would be linked with Raam, Ari's son. I offered Karel to bring the complete Artificial Intelligence unit of the Robinson Consortium, including its data bank and software. With Artificial Intelligence's application, we would begin without delay the development of programs such as human tissue cloning to produce the necessary organs for transplants; Three Dimension Printers for medical and industrial applications. We would be able to make from a dental piece to a car; and critical, interactive teaching systems for all levels. We could build a computerized system to achieve fair voting to elect government representatives.

"In the field of health, the possibilities are very encouraging; imagine a simple blood sample to determine the severe side effects a patient could suffer before taking a medication!

"Of course, it is essential to develop a cybersecurity system to prevent attacks from hackers.

"Raam is very excited about the prospects, and most grateful to us for having rescued him and having this new life.

"Ah! Your question, yes, of course, I also want to try a new life here!"

∾

Ikan and Shivon walked outside the mountain's cavity and descended to the canyon's bottom, where they found a river with clear water.

"Contemplate the beauty of this cliff, Shivon! We haven't lost anything; we continue to enjoy a place by a river in a private paradise!" His eyes sparkled, reflecting a mind full of daydreams.

"Karel asked me to work in close contact with him. He's concerned about the coal issue; its use to produce electricity in the world is one of the biggest pollutants in the atmosphere and responsible for global warming. We need to produce electricity with renewable sources such as solar, wind, tides, and hydrogen. The objective is to eliminate the use of coal within the next five years. The laboratories of Australia and Cambodia will be key to the implementation of wireless energy."

Ikan contemplated the undulating placid water of the river in front of them.

"The water invites for a dip! Are you in?"

∾

For several days, the group of newcomers participated in 'familiarization' sessions. The purpose of the sessions was a series of tests to assess their level of knowledge. After the tests, Karel apologized for having resorted to an objective evaluation of their abilities; It had to be done for the community's sake. On the other hand, he congratulated them for each one of them had exceeded the expected psychometric and technical marks. By way of 'relief' in a humorous tone, he offered them to officially present their 'graduation' to the community at a public ceremony.

Shortly after, the group gathered in one of the temporary rooms:

"We continue to interact as 'The Konnect Gang.' I imagine that at some point, once we assume our functions, our group will disintegrate in some way." Ariana conjectured.

"Not at all." Arthur winked at her with a smile.

"I agree." Ikan stood close to Shivon.

"I'm very grateful for my present situation," Ikan warned. "However, if there is a need to speak in public, don't count on me."

"I'm also out of consideration." Arthur clarified.

"What about Elisa speaking?" Ariana proposed. "I see her very equanimous, as usual."

The group voted, and everyone agreed. Elisa remained equanimous.

Epilogue

The auditorium in Xonnel was the cave of exceptional beauty the group had previously crossed. A high-tech sound system spread soft music evenly without any distortion. The community had met with enthusiasm, since social events didn't take place often. An innovative holographic system that worked as virtual reality without using a viewfinder projected large images at one end of the cave.

The music was interrupted, and from the stand, Karel welcomed the audience. His image appeared amplified in a holographic system.

"Three weeks ago, I had the pleasure of meeting Shivon, Elisa, Ariana, Ikan, Arthur, Ari, and Raam. They came to our community, guided by Achak. It was part of a chain of events linked for the good of all of us. The personal and professional qualities of our new members constitute a valuable contribution to our community. With their support, we will continue to meet the objectives of our mission.

"With you: Elisa."

The audience cheered.

"I thank you for coming, and I take this opportunity to refer to a subject I consider especially important:

Our identity.

"During our daily lives, we identify ourselves and others, by what we do; the engineer, the doctor, the musician, and not by who we really are.

"Practicing as a doctor is a temporary role; it doesn't define who the person really is. If somebody identifies himself with his circumstances, such as the challenges and problems that arise in his everyday activities, his spiritual nature, his true identity, is forgotten even more. In this process, he forgets his potential and his vast resources to overcome material conditions.

"Our world is experiencing challenging times. We came to Xonnel to stay out of the chaos that prevailed everywhere. We don't always understand the purpose of some changes; in the end, we must trust the result will be a step forward. The universe is continually expanding, creating, and evolving. There is no going back.

"Xonnel intends to act as the opposite of chaos, the opposite of negative energy. I could say that the path we walk during our human experience is illustrated in the Yin Yang symbol. In this symbol, the white part represents the positive energy which: integrates, connects, expands. The dark part represents the negative energy which: disconnects, segregates, frightens.

"Every human during the course on his path chooses to experience the polarity of Yin Yang:

"On the positive side: I feel safe, at peace, creative, I follow my intuition.

"The negative side is a deceiver; therefore, it uses stratagems to lure you because it doesn't reflect your true nature:

You are alone in the world.

You have no support.

You are useless, worthless.

This is going to be from bad to worse...

"Both poles are necessary because to know who you are, you need to compare yourself with something, to have a reference, compare yourself with what you are not.

"When we become aware of our spiritual nature, we understand that in the Yin Yang symbol, in addition to the positive pole (white) and negative pole (black), there is an intermediate zone of neutrality. This zone of neutrality is the one we should ideally stay on.

"From this area, we can observe the polarity and choose what we need to experience. We can be aware of the negative energy and its effects without fear, and therefore we don't have to experience it. When we manage to stay in this zone of neutrality, we manifest our true identity.

"I see pleasant surprises and gratifying accomplishments coming to Xonnel, not by having asked for it, but by how grateful we are!

Thank you for listening; enjoy the story of your life!

~

On the same night at the end of the ceremony, Ariana and Shivon dialogued in their room:

With a tone of nostalgia, Ariana expressed:

"Shivon, you know the story of our group better than anyone else. Would you write it if I asked you to?"

"I'd have to ask everyone's permission and gather some anecdotes."

"Tell me, would you really do it?"

"Yes, it would be our story."

"And what we experience here in Xonnel, would you narrate it too?"

"That would be another story. Someday I'll answer you."

END

ABOUT THE AUTHOR

Manuel Lanz

Manuel enjoys creative projects in his everyday life. He believes that purpose is created when he listens to the book that requests to be written, the image that calls to be painted, or the song that resonates inside him to be composed. The key element in these actions is creativity; when he creates, he finds meaning in the action,and he expresses who he is. Manuel has lived in several countries and appreciates their different cultures. In addition to his inclination for writing, his artistic works are represented in musical composition, photography ,and modern media art.

ABOUT THE ARTIST

Marcela Ewertz

Fine artist, Marcela Ewertz, channels her intuitive knowing into her paintings to metaphorically reflect as a mirror of her experiences. A Certified Clinical Hypnotherapist focuses on facilitating wellbeing to individuals, in body, mind, and emotions. With therapeutic imagery in hypnosis, Marcela helps to empower her clients in awakening their self-awareness for the fulfillment of their goals.

www.Marcela Ewertz.com (Art)

www.Marcela Ewertz.net (Hypnotherapy)